BRINGING HOME CHRISTMAS

VICKI HINZE

MAGNOLIA LEAF PRESS

Bringing Home Christmas

Published by Magnolia Leaf Press
Niceville, Florida, USA

Ebook ISBN: 978-1-939016-37-9
Print ISBN: 978-1-939016-36-2

Cover Design by VK Hinze

DEDICATION

For Nana, Mary and Linda,
All greatly admired. All deeply respected and appreciated. All an inspiration and endless source of hope and faith—proof of the goodness in people. May you always be blessed and known for the beacon of love and light you are for others.
With Love,
Vicki

BRINGING HOME CHRISTMAS

1

Atlanta, Georgia
December 18th
1:30 AM

SIRENS BLARED.

Lauren Holt punched at her pillows, her phone in her hand. In three years, she'd moved twice to get away from the traffic noise but discovered there were no apartments in the City of Atlanta that offered an escape. At least school was out for the holidays. Her third-grade class had been so excited, and they had loved the wooden-reindeer clothespin ornaments she'd made for them.

Christmas at home in Holt Ridge, Tennessee, had been her favorite time of year. But living alone in Atlanta left her with no family nearby and no festivities to celebrate. That, of course, brought to mind the reason for her isolation—David Decker.

So close. She'd come so close to marrying him. Then in

the week before their wedding, he had shattered her world. Why had he done that?

Still having no idea, she rested back against the pillows then tapped her phone screen, hoping somehow she'd hear something in his last voice mail she hadn't heard in the past three years.

"Lauren, it's David. The negotiations are going well to resolve the last-minute dispute. I should wrap up tomorrow morning and be on a flight tomorrow night. I'm the luckiest man alive. In three days, you'll be my wife. I love you. We're going to build a great life together. I can't wait. Night, angel."

She let out a wistful sigh. His eager tone. No hint of cold feet or of anything being wrong. *A great life together. Love.* Her heart hitched and a lump swelled in her throat. How had so much changed in just two days?

As baffled now as then, she stared at the screen. Tapped the messages and scrolled to his last text. The one he had sent her the night before their wedding...

LAUREN, I'M SORRY ABOUT THE TIMING ON THIS, BUT I've decided our marriage would be a mistake. I can't do that to either of us. I hope you will be happy and find the right man for you. When I return, it will be to Nashville, not to Holt Ridge.

A MISTAKE. FROM *LOVE* AND *A GREAT LIFE TOGETHER* TO *A mistake. How? Why?*

Having no answers, she sighed her frustration. Her chest tight, her heart weary, she set the phone on the bedside table and clicked off the lamp, inhaling deeply the fresh scent of the cool, sun-dried sheets. Just like every other night in the past three years, she had listened and found no answers. Not in his voice mail. Not in his text. Not in her broken heart.

Her mother advised Lauren repeatedly to move on, to fall in love again. But how could she even try? Why would she want to try? The costs of loving were steep. A broken heart incapable of healing, constant haunting memories of all the good that had been lost. Logically, she knew she should move on. Realistically, it was impossible to do.

She was stuck. Torn between imagining what their life together would have been like and wondering if she'd ever really known David at all. He'd deserted her the night before their wedding in a text message. A text message. What kind of man did that?

December 19th
3:00 AM

The phone rang.

Lauren startled awake and snagged it, checked caller ID. *Caroline?* Why would her sister be calling her at this time of night? Had to be bad news. "Hello."

"Lauren, it's me." Caroline's voice cracked. "It's Mom."

Lauren sat straight up in bed, bunched the covers in a closed fist. "What's wrong with her?" She'd had surgery a couple days ago. Routine, Caroline had said. And it had gone well.

"She's developed a post-operative infection." Caroline paused. "It happens sometimes, they say, but she's not responding to treatment."

"Did you ask Jessica about it?" Lauren asked. Jessica Weaver had been Lauren's best friend all her life. She was an excellent nurse.

"I did. She's taking care of mom, just like you asked," Caroline said. "Lauren, it's bad. Really bad. Jessica says they're doing all they can, but nothing is working. She said we'd better be prepared."

Lauren tried to swallow a gasp, reminded herself to breathe.

"Mom said to call you." Caroline sniffled, exhaled a sharp breath that blew static through the phone. "She said she wants to see you…one more time."

One more time? Lauren swung her feet over the edge of the bed, toe-seeking her slippers. "I'll see if I can get a flight."

"A week before Christmas?" Caroline grunted. "That's going to be impossible."

"Maybe, but I'm going to try," Lauren said. "I have to try."

"We're having heavy snow storms, too."

"It always snows there this time of year," Lauren let her impatience seep into her voice. "Stop worrying, Caroline. One way or another, I'll get there. You tell Mom, I'm coming."

"I will." Caroline cleared her throat. "Lauren, I'm scared."

Caroline was the older sister but her being the protective one in real life had never worked. Since their father's sudden death when they were twelve and ten, Lauren had been the one to step up and try to right the wrongs and fix whatever happened to break to keep them and their mother glued together. Their dad had made a hairpin turn on an icy mountain road and slid into a ravine. Caroline, who had always been closer to him, had been devastated by his death. She'd become a semi-recluse, hidden away with her books, and she seemed content to stay that way. The truth was Caroline, while genuinely devastated, also liked nature and animals more than people. If she had to feign devastation indefinitely and being inept to get more time alone and less with others, she had no qualms with doing it.

How their mother hadn't seen through Caroline's convenient ineptitude was beyond Lauren, though honestly, Mom never had seen what she chose not to see in anyone, including in her daughters.

Little sobs crackled through the phone. Lauren's heart tugged. "Caroline, it's going to be okay. Hold yourself together, all right?"

"All right." She paused. "I'm so glad you're coming home."

"Of course, I'm coming home. Have either of you ever needed me and I haven't come?"

"Well, no, but I worried this time might be different."

"Why?"

"Because of David."

Lauren stilled at her bedside. "What has he got to do with this?"

Caroline hesitated. "You know. You haven't been back home once since you left. Your leaving was all about him and we all know it."

David was the last thing Lauren wanted to talk about right now. "I'd better get busy trying for a flight. Tell Mom we talked and what I said. I'll be there as soon as I can…"

2

Holt Ridge, Tennessee
December 19th
9:30 PM

THE COMMUNITY HOSPITAL was decorated for Christmas. Visiting hours were over, but Lauren entered through the Emergency Room and headed straight for the surgical wing on the second floor and then walked on to the nurse's station. Becky Grayson sat behind the desk, charting and looking the same as she had when Lauren had been ten. "Mrs. Grayson?"

"Lauren." She smiled and stood up. "Oh, I'm glad you're here. Your mom has been so excited about you coming." She dropped her voice. "She was afraid, I think, you wouldn't."

Again? Just like Caroline. "Why wouldn't I come? My mother is ill."

"David, of course." The unflappable Mrs. Grayson

shrugged. "I told her, if she needed you, wild horses wouldn't keep you away. But she still worried."

They moved down the hall as they spoke, and she stopped outside a room. Lauren stopped beside her. "Is she doing any better?"

"Not yet." Empathy shone in Mrs. Grayson's eyes. "But seeing you might be just the thing she needs."

"Is she going to..." Lauren couldn't make herself say the word die. But her mother's *one more time* had reverberated in her head over and again since Caroline had first relayed it.

"The antibiotics will kick in. Sometimes it takes a while," Mrs. Grayson avoided giving an easy yes or no answer. "I know it's hard, but this kind of infection is hard on her heart and her kidneys, Lauren. We're just going to have to wait and see and hope."

Hope. Lauren could hope. She nodded. "Thank you." She meant it sincerely.

Mrs. Grayson nodded and pushed the door open. "Vanessa, look who's here."

Lauren stepped into the hospital room and tried to hide her shock. Her mother, always pristine and particular with her appearance, looked like a shadow of her former self. Her dark hair was loose and unbrushed, her cheeks sunken. She looked old and frail and dark shadows circled her intelligent eyes. "Hi, Mom."

"Lauren." She lifted her hand. The other rested on a pillow at her side, an IV hooked to a stand behind her head with three bags of fluids that steadily dripped through the tube and into her arm. "I'm so glad you're home."

Lauren bent and dropped a kiss to her mother's forehead, struggled to control her emotions at seeing her mother in this condition. "I got here as soon as I could."

"Caroline told me you'd come. I wasn't sure, but she said you would even if you had to walk."

Lauren smiled. "She was right."

"She was." She patted the mattress beside her. "Sit."

"Better not," Lauren said, dropping her handbag to the floor. She stepped over to the sink and washed her hands with hot water and lots of soap. "I've been on a plane most of the day. No telling what kind of germs were on it."

"You're right." Her mother paused. "I guess the last thing I need is more germs."

"Exactly." Lauren grabbed two towelettes from the dispenser and dried her hands, then tossed them into the trash. "So how did this surgery go from a simple little procedure to a raging infection?"

"If I knew the answer to that, would I have let it happen?" Her mother arched a brow.

"No, I guess you wouldn't." Lauren smiled.

The door opened. "I'm sending down for sandwiches," Mrs. Grayson said. "Don't bother telling me you're not hungry, Vanessa. I'm not having it. Lauren's got to be half-starved and she has never liked eating alone so you'll have to eat with her." Mrs. Grayson winked at Lauren. "What kind would you like?"

Lauren guessed this had to do with her mother not eating since Lauren lived and ate alone all the time and had for three years. Truthfully, she did still hate it. At first, she'd had to make herself eat. Then she kind of got used to it. But she still hated it. She glanced at her Mom. "Turkey?"

Her mother nodded. "Fine."

Lauren savored the small victory. "Turkey with mayo for me. Mom loves turkey with cranberry, if there's any in the kitchen. Mom can't abide mayonnaise."

"Well, that's a handy piece of information to know," Mrs. Grayson said. "You should have told me, Vanessa."

"I didn't want to be a bother."

"Be a bother." Mrs. Grayson frowned. "You must eat to keep up your strength."

"Then strengthen me with some potato chips, too."

"I can make that happen. Low salt."

"Fine."

Lauren grinned. "She's not a fan of low salt, but if you throw in a piece of pie…"

"Pumpkin or apple?"

"Apple," Mom said.

"No ice-cream," Lauren added. "A little melted cheddar. It's her favorite."

"Got it." Mrs. Grayson nodded and withheld a smile that touched her eyes. "Be right back."

As soon as the door closed, her mother reached for Lauren's hand. "I hate seeing you look so worried."

They had always been blunt and brutally honest with each other. Seeing no reason to change that now, Lauren admitted, "I am worried."

"It's bad. I can feel it."

"How bad?" she asked. "Are you going to die, Mom?" Lauren looked her mother right in the eye. "Or are you going to fight this infection and live?"

Her mother reached for her hand and squeezed her fingers. "I'm going to fight."

"Good." Lauren shuddered relief. Her mother might not commit to living, but she had committed to fighting. That's all Lauren could ask. "What can I do to help?"

"This is a battle I have to fight alone, but there is something else weighing on my mind. If you could do something about that, it would stop me worrying about it."

"What is it, Mom?"

"The annual Christmas dinner and dance. I'm chair again this year."

"You're chair every year."

"Exactly," she said, as if that explained her concern. "No one else knows what to do, except for you. You helped me with it for years."

The Christmas dinner and dance was for adults and kids, a big fundraiser in the community that benefited the school's music program. Music had always been a big part of her mom's life. She was determined to keep it available for the kids. "I did help you with it."

"Often, and Caroline, well, bless her heart, she's just not organizationally gifted."

She was a librarian and extraordinarily organized, when she wanted to be. "Not if it means she has to interact with other people."

Her mother nodded. "Especially then."

She knew exactly what Caroline had been doing.

"Lauren, you know how important the dinner and dance is to the community."

"I know. The music program is totally reliant on it."

"Exactly," her mom said. "I'm afraid this medical nonsense has interrupted my work."

"You need me to step in and take care of it for you," Lauren said. The majority of the work was typically done by Thanksgiving. It couldn't be that bad. "Well, I am off from school until after the holidays. I can do that for you. You stop worrying about any of it, and just focus on getting well."

"Thank you, sweetheart. I appreciate it." Her mom seemed genuinely relieved. "You'll have to oversee the parade, and the bonfire, of course, but Barbara and Kenneth Pope will help." Her face clouded. "And there are others."

Barbara Pope had been her mother's friend and florist forever, and her husband, Kenneth, was the best caterer in the county. How many times had she told Lauren that she and David reminded Barbara of her and Kenneth at their ages? At least a couple dozen. "Others?"

The door opened and Mrs. Grayson entered with a tray. "Here we go." She passed a tray to Lauren and set the second on the bedside table, then raised the head of Vanessa's bed. "Do try to get this down," she said. "You haven't eaten enough to keep a bird alive in three days."

"I will," her mom promised. "I have to. If I don't, Lauren will accuse me of not fighting."

Mrs. Grayson looked pleased with that answer. "Then let's don't disappoint her," she said. "Poor lamb has been disappointed enough."

Lauren's face burned at the reminder of David's desertion. Three years, and no one had forgotten. They'd killed her with kindness and unintended barbs before she'd gotten enough of it and left for Atlanta. Now it seemed she was in for another round.

But her mother was eating.

For her mother to eat and get strong and fight to live, Lauren could take another round. Even more…

3

December 19th
11:30 PM

LAUREN ENTERED the home office that once had been her father's. The scent of old wood, lemon oil polish on the desk, the high-back wing chair across from it, and the leather sofa against the far wall brought back vivid memories of her standing at the door, peeking in, seeing Caroline leaning back against the sofa arm, her legs curled up and her nose buried in a book, and their father sitting in his office chair, his nose buried in paperwork. Lauren could still hear the tip of his pen scratching slashes of red across the pages.

The two of them would stay in his office for hours and hours. And now and then, Lauren would stand at the door and look in and then go on her way to do whatever it was she needed to do that evening. Dad and Caroline had been two peas in a pod. Lauren hadn't fit in with them. She loved them, and they loved her. She just wasn't like them.

She and her mother always had more in common. They'd bake and garden and do craft projects together in her studio out in the backyard. And they'd work on her mother's charitable projects, like the Christmas dinner and dance. Vanessa Holt took those responsibilities very seriously, and she always had. Whether that was due to Dad's grandfather being the founder of Holt Ridge and her mother maintaining his standing in the community though he was long gone, Lauren had never asked. But knowing her mother, it was her family duty to assure that the Holt name was honored and respected. She'd always been protective of it, reminding her girls that their behavior reflected not just on them but the family and the community. Caroline shrugged off those lessons, but Lauren took them in deep. There was something comforting in them. A sense of purpose and belonging.

She moved to the desk and pulled open the bottom left drawer, where her mother said the file on the dinner and dance could be found. Lauren pulled it out, thinking it was awfully thin. Typically, her mother had done the majority of the work for the dance before Thanksgiving, and she documented everything. This close to Christmas, the file was usually a half-inch thick.

Lauren opened the file on the desktop and looked inside, scanning the mostly blank pages. "What is this?" Nothing. The plans were not even all there. Not a word on the volunteers. Nothing on the annual sleigh ride or the Critter Christmas Parade which culminated with the community bonfire and caroling—all traditions that took place the afternoon and evening before the Christmas dinner and dance.

Caroline came in and sat down, her pajamas a soft blue

flannel. "What are you doing in here? I thought you'd be dead on your feet tonight."

"I am, but I'm too wired to sleep." Lauren looked over at her sister, sitting in the wingback chair. "Mom asked me to help her with the Christmas events."

"She asked me, too." Caroline groaned. "I wisely reminded her I was the last person she wanted to do any of it."

Convenient ineptitude. "You invoked the family reputation, didn't you?"

"I did." Caroline shot Lauren a cheeky grin. "Whatever it takes." She lifted a hand and wagged a finger at the file. "You know this stuff is not my thing."

"She's sick, Caroline. See-you-one-last-time sick."

"I know that. I didn't want to make her sicker by upsetting her. You know how crazy she gets about this stuff—perfection on steroids—and I really am lousy at it."

Lauren couldn't disagree. Instead, she sighed. "She's usually a lot further along in the planning. There isn't a single checklist in her whole file." A thought struck and stayed. "How long has she been sick?" Must have been a lot longer than Caroline had told Lauren before the surgery.

"Since late September. But not straight through. She had attacks now and then but otherwise, she was doing okay, or I would have told you."

Not looking her in the eye. She'd been sworn to secrecy about it. "So, if she was doing okay most of that time, why is nothing done on the planning?"

"I can't answer that." Caroline hesitated. "But maybe her co-chair can."

"Mom has a co-chair?" Her mother had never had a co-chair on this project or any other.

Caroline nodded, licked at her lips, far from comfortable. "She thought it might help him integrate into the community—and apparently she was right. It has."

Deliberately avoiding disclosing his identity. Typical Caroline. She ran from confrontation as if demons were chasing her heels. But she wouldn't lie, if asked the right question in a direct manner that left her no wiggle room. "Who is the co-chair?"

Before answering, Caroline stood and moved halfway to the door. "Um, David."

Lauren searched her memory, but she couldn't think of anyone in the community named David. Wait. Caroline had said integrate. "David," she repeated. "David…who?"

Caroline inched closer to the doorway. "David Decker, Lauren."

Lauren's jaw fell open. Her ex-fiancé? Why? And why would her mother help him integrate into the community? Her mother hadn't been crazy about David when he and Lauren had been engaged. He was an outsider and she feared he'd take Lauren away from Holt Ridge. "What is David Decker doing here?" The last Lauren had heard from her best friend, Jessica, he was working for a security firm out of Nashville.

"I don't know, and that's the truth. No one knows why he came here, only that he did." Caroline leaned against the door frame. "If I were him, this would be the last place on the planet I'd come."

Lauren was with Caroline on that one. "I don't understand. He has no family or roots here." Lauren didn't like this. Not at all. Alarms blared inside her mind. "Of all the towns in the country, why did he have to choose mine?"

"There's been a lot of speculation on that," Caroline admitted. "Like you said, he has no family or friends here. And his ditching you the night before your wedding…well, that didn't exactly endear him to people around here."

All the gossip and tongue wagging had sent Lauren to Atlanta. She couldn't take it anymore, or their pitying looks. She'd hoped their interest would die down, but it didn't. It got worse. It all became just too much. *Poor Lauren Holt. Dumped the night before the wedding, and the groom left not just the town or the state to get away from her, but the whole country.* Her face went hot and her throat tight. When she could, she asked, "So he lives here now, and Mom has him as a co-chair on the Christmas festivities?"

Caroline nodded. "That's about it."

"No, that's far from it." Why was he here? Rubbing her nose in it wasn't his style, but what else was left? What he'd done already hadn't been enough to satisfy him? He wanted more? "How long has he lived here?"

With a lift of her shoulder, Caroline estimated. "About two years, I'd say. It was right before Memorial Day. I remember because it was the first time I saw him on Main Street. All the flags for the local soldiers who'd passed away while in the service were out. You know how they line the street at town circle."

"Two years?" Shock rippled through Lauren. "And you didn't tell me?"

"Mom didn't tell you either."

"Why?" A deep sense of betrayal swelled in Lauren. "How could either of you not tell me?"

"I didn't because Mom said not to," Caroline told her. "I don't know what her reasons were, but I'm sure she thought she was protecting you."

"You should have told me, Caroline," Lauren said. "You're my sister."

"Sorry. She made me promise."

And Caroline was slow to make promises, but she always kept them.

Her emotions in riot, Lauren stared off at a spot on the

far wall and ordered them to settle down. "He's a global security consultant. What does he do in Holt Ridge?" A community of a couple thousand people left only the wildlife, and they didn't need his services.

"David has his own company. Red Cedar Global Security."

This made no sense. None. Lauren feared asking but she needed to know. "Is he alone?"

"He is." Caroline nodded. "It hasn't been easy for him. Actually, he had a rough start. Everybody around here was pretty upset with him…well, you know."

"About cancelling the wedding," Lauren filled in the blanks.

"Well, yeah. They shunned him," Caroline said. "But he kept coming back for more, inserting himself into the community, and he's been very active. Mom helped with that. You know how she loves underdogs. Anyway, now he's wormed his way in as a local."

While Lauren remained stuck in isolation in Atlanta. No family, no friends, no home and nothing familiar. He'd ditched her. Why did he get her community and she get nothing? This was just wrong. Just wrong.

She shut the file and then stood up. "Well, you're going to have to do the Christmas festivities for Mom. There's no way I'm working with David Decker on anything."

"No."

Lauren frowned at her sister. "What do you mean, no?"

"No means no. I'm not doing it. Mom asked you, you agreed, and that's that." Caroline turned into the hall and walked away. "Deal with it, Lauren."

Lauren followed her. "I can't believe you're doing this to me. You know people are talking about this already. You know every bit of what happened is all back now and they're gossiping about it all over again."

"They are. But it'll pass." Caroline didn't so much as look back. "I can't do this for you. I'm horrible at this kind of thing and you know it. Mom and the kids counting on a decent music program deserve better than me. They deserve you."

"You're really going to do this to me?"

"I'm not doing anything to you."

Lauren snapped her jaw shut. "This is not over, Caroline."

"It is for me." She turned the corner and disappeared from sight, leaving a flustered Lauren rattled and shaken and even a little angry at her family and her community. How could they betray her and embrace her biggest betrayer?

She slapped at the light switch. The lamp went out. There was only one logical reason David Decker would come here. To taunt her. And he must want to do it pretty badly. She hadn't been back here in three years. One would think he'd have given up and left long before now. But not David. He was as tenacious as a bulldog.

Well, if he thought he was going to get a rise out of her, he had another thought coming. Her devastation days were over. His return had changed all the rules. It had changed everything…

4

December 20th
9:30 AM

AT THE HOSPITAL, Lauren checked in with the nurse on duty, Sandra Mason. They'd had classes together in high school, though her hair had been brown then and not streaked blond. It looked good on her.

"Your mom had a reasonably good night, but her numbers aren't improving, Lauren," she said. "The longer this goes on, the weaker she's getting."

"What does Dr. Fleming say?" Lauren asked, adjusting her purse strap on her shoulder. "I'd hoped to see him on rounds this morning."

"He was in early today," Sandra said. "The infection is spreading, and the more it spreads, the worse her odds are for successfully fighting it off."

What wasn't said hit Lauren hard. She'd known, of course, there was a chance her mother wouldn't survive this, but hearing Sandra articulate that frightened her in ways she couldn't begin to explain, much less digest. "I see."

"She did eat half a sandwich last night. That's a good sign."

"I was here," Lauren said. "Can I go see her?"

"Sure. Just don't tire her out."

"I won't." Lauren turned and walked to her mother's room, reminding herself to breathe, to not let her see Lauren's concern. She would be watching for signs. She'd always watched for signs on whether or not she should be worried.

Lauren eased the door open and peeked inside. Her mother looked so small in the hospital bed with tubes running from her arms to an IV stand behind her. The constant beep of a heart monitor was oddly reassuring. Her eyes were closed.

Lauren slipped inside and took a seat beside her bed. Just stared at her mother's brave face. Memories flooded her. The police arriving at home, telling them they'd found Dad's car. That he had crashed into the ravine and had not survived. The grief at the funeral, how quiet her mother had been for months afterward, sitting alone in the dark, staring into space as if seeing things that no one else could see.

Months had passed and winter had given way to summer, and that's when the adventures had begun. Learning to drive the riding mower, washing the cars, the mega water fight with the hose. How strange the first laughter had been after the long months of silent sobbing, snared in the merciless vice of grief. Her utter delight at her irises blooming, coming home from school to blaring music and finding her mother in her She Shack, the old studio out back, painting for the first time in years.

She'd loved Dad with all her heart. But that day, Lauren realized that her mother would not only be okay, she'd be her whole self again in a new way. One where she alone defined her life. It was a startling realization that she had denied things that made her happy to please her father.

"Lauren?" Her mother called out to her. "Why didn't you wake me?"

"Sleep is healing time," Lauren said. "Isn't that what you always told me?"

She nodded, reached for her daughter's hand. "Stop looking so worried. I'm all right."

"That's good to hear."

"I decided last night I'm tired of feeling like this. I promised myself if I woke up today, I wasn't going to let this infection beat me."

"Good. I can stop worrying then." When her mother made her mind, that was that.

She sent Lauren a sidelong look. "I take it you spoke to Caroline and she told you David is here."

Caroline had called her. Not a doubt in Lauren's mind. "She did. But let's don't talk about him. Let's focus on getting you well."

"I am getting well," she countered. "I told you, I decided."

"Okay." Lauren agreed to not upset her.

"So, Caroline did tell you all about David. Good, that's settled then."

"Not exactly," Lauren said. "She didn't tell me was why he's here." Did her mother know?

She smoothed her hair with a blue-veined hand. "I suppose you're upset because I didn't tell you."

"It is curious that neither you nor Caroline told me." Jessica Weaver hadn't told Lauren either, and they spoke at least every other Saturday. It was an agreed upon conspiracy. They happened now and then on the Ridge. "I suppose that was deliberate, and you made the call. Am I right?"

She turned her head on the pillow, her hair rustling against its slip. "Deliberate and intentional. I gave the matter a lot of thought and decided it was best left alone."

"Mom, I should have known."

"And now you do."

Couldn't argue that. Lauren had tossed and turned half the night, only too well aware. "It won't matter, but it must be said. That wasn't your decision to make. Keeping it from me, I mean."

"That's debatable." She blinked, then blinked again. "But let's save it for another time."

"Okay." That was best. She didn't want her mother upset.

"What else do you want to know?"

Everything, but not now. "I want you well."

"Questions about David, Lauren."

Why was she pushing this? Clearly, she was determined. "Do you know why he came here, or moved his company here?"

"Only David knows that," her mother said.

If her mother didn't know, no one knew. She'd have dragged the truth out of anyone else in the county. "It wasn't a sensible thing for him to do," Lauren said. "I thought he was a sensible man."

"He is a sensible man," her mother agreed. "But even sensible men do foolish things sometimes. Of course, they don't see them as foolish when they do them. To them, their reasons make perfect sense."

"Well, whatever his reasons, they don't matter anymore. Not to me." She knew deep down in places so close to the bone she couldn't speak of them out loud that he'd had a specific reason for coming here. The wounded woman in her thought to humiliate her, but that would be so unlike him. Maybe her humiliation was the net effect, yet she couldn't see him setting out to deliberately do that to her or anyone else.

Odds were, he had no idea how much he'd humiliated her already. If he had known, maybe he would have stayed in Nashville. Either way, he was here, and she was done. His days of humiliating her unintentionally or deliberately were over.

Yet she would still like to know why he had broken their engagement the night before their wedding. In a text.

She bit her lip to stave off a frown. Three years of listening to his last voice mail. Reading his last text. Neither had solved the puzzle. But he could answer her questions and end the haunting.

"Not to be stepping on your toes, dear, but if you'd come home before now, then you would have known he was here. You didn't."

"True." It was, as far as it went. Deep down, she didn't want to talk to David. The time for that had passed long ago. And yet, she deserved to know why. She was weary of wondering about it. Who wouldn't want answers? "But I'm here now."

"Then perhaps you should ask him your questions."

To get answers and move on. Close that chapter of her life. "Perhaps I should."

"The committee has an 11:00 meeting at Community Hall. If you hurry, you won't be late."

Lauren glanced at her watch. 10:45. "I'll come again afterward."

"Maybe after you ask David your questions."

"Maybe so." What if she got those answers and

learned it was all her fault? That would be hard to take, but it would be better to know.

"Lauren," her mother reached for her hand. "As a kindness to me, please don't cause a scene with David today. It would embarrass me to tears."

Nobody did guilt as well as her mother. And no one stuck to decorum like her, either. "I won't cause a scene, Mom."

"Thank you, dear."

Lauren dropped a kiss on her cool forehead. No fever. That was a good sign. "You fight to get well, Mom. Really fight. And eat."

Her mother nodded then closed her eyes to rest.

Lauren left the room and closed the door behind her. When she turned, she was looking right into Jessica Weaver's smiling face. Her ebony skin glowed, and her hair had been snipped short. Lauren smiled and wrapped her arms around Jessica's neck. "You look fabulous."

"Wearing love on the outside," she said, swiping an arm down her blue scrubs, her stethoscope dangling from her neck, tucked into her pocket. "Want to meet him?"

Lauren smiled. "Of course."

A tall man wearing boots and a cowboy hat joined them. Jessica wrapped her arm in his. "Jason, this is my best friend, Lauren Holt. Lauren, my guy, Jason."

They chatted briefly, then Jason said, "I'm sorry. I'm late for an appointment. Lauren, I'm glad you're home. Jessica has been waiting for you to come back for a long time."

"Thank you." Lauren watched him walk away. "He's gorgeous, Jess."

"He is." Jessica let out a dreamy sigh.

Lauren smiled, unable to resist a little taunting. "So, she who swore since third grade she would never be interested in a guy who wore a cowboy hat and boots—does he drive a truck?"

Jessica laughed. "He does!" She dropped her voice. "We star gaze from the backend all the time out at Miller's Creek."

"Well, you got to eat all your words, then."

"I did." She chuckled. "Isn't that the biggest blessing ever?"

"If it puts that kind of happiness on your face, then I'd say it certainly is."

"I'm crazy about him. The miracle is he's crazy about me, too."

Lauren clasped her arm. "I'm so happy for you."

"I know you are." Jessica looked over her shoulder. "Boss is back. I've got to run. Let's do dinner tonight at Granny's. Seven okay?"

"Perfect." Granny's was an institution in Holt Ridge. It'd been the first business to open on Main Street. Granny's granddaughter ran it now—or she had three years ago, when Lauren had left, and her dad, Bailey Adams, owned it. "See you then." Two steps down the hall, Lauren paused. "Jess?"

She stopped, turned back, and waited.

"You should have told me he was here." No need to mention David's name. The suddenly sober expression on Jessica's face proved she knew exactly who Lauren meant.

"I would have, if I'd known you were coming back."

"Why didn't you tell me when it happened?"

Jessica shifted on her feet. "Because you would have felt betrayed by everyone on the ridge, including your mother, and by him all over again."

She did anyway. Jessica was right, though. Knowing he had usurped her life here and she was now the outsider would have made Lauren more miserable in Atlanta. At least, she'd just been wondering what had happened. She hadn't been clueless *and* betrayed. Being both was definitely worse. "See you at seven."

Jessica walked on, and Lauren checked her watch. She had three minutes to get to Community Hall. She wouldn't make it by eleven, but that was fine. David Decker could just wait.

At least, he wouldn't have to cancel a wedding and then face the entire community alone. Remembering how hard that had been, how much it had hurt, she couldn't wish that experience on anyone. Not even him.

5

December 20th
11:00 AM

LIGHT SNOW DUSTED the crusted pack on the shallow lawns of the businesses and municipal offices at Town Circle. Lauren dipped her chin into the scarf draping her neck, her hands stuffed deep in her pockets, and made her way down the sidewalk to Community Hall. The rockers, barrel table and checkerboard stood empty, which was common this time of year. At the door, she stomped her snow boots on the mat, then went inside.

The main hall was a flurry of activity. Familiar people decorating an enormous Christmas tree, admiring their handy-work. A woman who looked from the back like Mrs. Grayson placed wrapped packages with gold and silver ribbons under the tree atop the red velvet skirt. Men moving out the sofas and chairs that typically filled the space, and more men moving in circular tables that would be placed around the perimeter of the wide room, leaving the far third for a dance floor. Across the hardwood floor, in that far third area, a long table stood. Six committee members sat in chairs around it. Barbara and Kenneth Pope, their beloved and spoiled rotten dog, Baxter, and at the head of the table, David Decker.

He wore a black suit and tie, white shirt, and a scruffy beard that looked great on him. His face was thinner, more angular; he'd lost maybe fifteen pounds, not that he'd needed to, and his hair was darker, nearly black. No sun-streaks in it now. He looked… amazing. She wanted to deny it but couldn't. Reminding herself to breathe, Lauren walked across the expanse to the foot of the table. "Hello, everyone." She focused on the Popes. "I see you're doing well, Baxter." She bent to ruffle his scruff.

"Welcome home, Lauren." Barbara laughed. "The scamp is nagging us for a quick walk." Barbara stood up. "Kenneth, you'd best come too, in case he decides to make a run for it."

"Good to see you home, Lauren." Kenneth stood up. "We won't be long."

The other committee members grabbed the opportunity to freshen up their coffee and run to the restroom. Truth be told, Lauren knew they expected fireworks between David and she and they were getting out of the line of fire. Lauren stiffened her back. Neither they nor he would be getting that from her, and likely not from David. At least, if he was anything like she thought he had been. But he was here. Who knew anymore what to expect?

When only the two of them remained at the table, David greeted her. "Hello, Lauren."

"David." She spotted a walking cane hooked on the arm of his chair. Had he pulled a muscle or something?

"I hope your being here isn't a sign your mother has taken a turn for the worse."

Civil. She could be civil. The cane handle looked a little worn. Had he been using it a while, or was it issued to him at the hospital? "She isn't responding to the antibiotics yet, but she is eating a little again. That's a good sign." Lauren feigned a smile. "Thank you for asking."

"Baxter!" Barbara Pope's shout echoed through the large room.

Lauren glanced over and saw Baxter standing staring at Barbara with a gold-ribboned package dangling from his mouth.

Barbara pointed a finger and barked an order. "You take that back right this minute, young man."

The dog tucked his tail tucked, turned, and headed back to the tree. He dropped the package and sat down, no doubt waiting for Barbara to turn her back so he could snitch it again.

Some things never change. Baxter getting into trouble was one of them.

"Kenneth," Barbara called to her husband, standing nearby. "Check his mouth and make sure he didn't cut his lip on that ribbon."

"Yes, dear."

David chuckled. "They treat that dog better than most do people."

"He's like a child to them." The Popes were crazy about Baxter, and that he was a mischievous rascal entertained them.

"Gathered that a long time ago," David said. "He's annoying, but there's something about him..."

"He's endearing," Lauren finished for him. "He's always been that way. No matter how much trouble he gets into, you just can't stay upset with him."

"It's a gift."

"It has been to the Popes." Lauren sighed. "After Janelle passed away, they were lost, and so sad. But then Ollie Mae Baker's dog had pups and Baxter was the runt. She asked Kenneth and Barbara to take care of him. The others were picking on him, and being the runt, he couldn't defend himself."

"Sounds like a setup."

"It was," Lauren said. "But it worked anyway. They brought Baxter home and spoiled him rotten and they all healed."

"Who was Janelle?"

"Their daughter. She was at college in Kentucky. Driving home, she got a flat. You know the roadside hazards of that." Lauren blew out a steady breath. "She died instantly."

"Tragic," he said.

"It was." Lauren looked away.

"So, people don't get riled by Baxter's antics. Makes sense. Ridgers do tend to protect their own."

"Most of the time." That he was sitting at the other end of the table proved that wasn't always the case.

Questions of why he was here burned in her mind, but she tamped them down. The best way to deal with this—with him—was to stick to committee business. "I reviewed my mother's plans and I'm hoping yours are more complete. What's been done, and what is left that needs doing?"

He shifted on his seat. "Bluntly put, the plans are a train wreck." He swiped a hand through his hair. "When your mother told me that she had to have surgery, I stepped up on my side of things. I thought she had her side well in hand. Everyone said she was typically done by Thanksgiving. But apparently this year, she wasn't."

"I'm discovering she's been ill longer than anyone realized," Lauren said. "What exactly is your side of things?"

"Organizing the volunteers. Handling setups and breakdowns, and laying out the sleigh ride route with Bailey Adams, making sure it is safe."

"For?"

"The dinner and dance, the sleigh ride, the bonfire, the critter parade. And the Circle tree." He tilted his head in a way that was endearingly familiar. "That's done. The volunteers all have their marching orders."

"That's good news," she said. "So, what isn't done?"

"Everything else." He frowned, creasing the skin between his eyebrows. "Some things have been started, they're just not finished."

"Like what?"

"The dinner and dance tickets haven't been printed. Barbara agreed to do the flowers, but the order isn't finalized or approved. Kenneth's doing the catering, but the menu hasn't been finalized or approved. He's about out of time on ordering in, especially with the storms." David passed her a list. "Nothing on this is final."

"Why didn't you just sign off on it all?"

"Couldn't," he said. "Everything requires two signatures. I couldn't very well bother your mother with it, and she hadn't designated her replacement. Well, until now. I'm assuming you are replacing her. Why else would you be here?"

"I am filling in for her." This was so unlike her mother. But with her health issues, she wasn't herself. "What's top priority?"

"Everything." He frowned again. "It's only three days, Lauren—two until the bonfire, sleigh rides and the critter parade."

"Are the vendors set for the events?"

"They are. Just waiting for your signature."

She motioned for the document. Scanned it, spotted all the usual names for all the usual purposes, and signed off. "What's next?"

He paused to think a second. "I'm most concerned about the ticket sales for the dinner and dance. They're really slow."

"If they haven't been printed yet for people to buy them, that's why they're slow."

"Of course." He swallowed a sip of what had to be cold coffee. "Businesses around town have been having people sign up with ticket lists—so when the tickets are delivered, they can just pick them up. But sales are still slow compared to previous years." He looked down at the table. "I'm hoping it's not because I'm involved."

Clearly, he wanted reassurance. The wounded, angry part of her wanted to withhold it but, having been on the receiving end of that kind of thing one time too many, she didn't. "I'm sure it's not. They want the actual tickets in their hands," she said. "The dance is still a family affair, right?"

He nodded. "Dinner and dancing, people of all ages—and this year, formal."

"Formal?" That surprised Lauren. "The dance has never been formal."

"Community voted. The women wanted a chance to dress up." He looked back through his notes. "Most of the men opposed—on the first round of votes. But some swung the other way on the second round." He shrugged. "I'm guessing influences were exerted." He cleared his throat. "It was a very robust debate."

Lauren couldn't help it. She smiled. "Just for the sake of curiosity, how many rounds of votes did it take for the women to get their formal?"

"Three." He grunted. "They were persistent and persuasive."

"I'm sure they were."

"Well, I guess the wisest place to start is to review your documents and then get to the printer. Is Carter Slade still running the shop?"

David's relief was evident. "He is, and we have a meeting with him at two o'clock."

More time with David. Lauren buried her reaction.

"Would you like to grab some lunch?" he asked. "I could answer any questions…"

The invitation surprised her. She would, of course, refuse. Tongues would be blazing before their order was taken. "Better not. I think I need to get somewhere quiet and go through all this. I'll meet you at Carter's at 2:00."

6

December 20th
2:15 PM

DAVID RUSHED into Carter's print shop looking flustered. Scraggly bits of cotton stuck to his coat. "Sorry I'm late."

"What happened?" Lauren plucked a couple bits from his sleeve.

"I was on my way out, and Baxter decided to rip the stuffing out of Santa—the stuffed one. What a mess."

"What about Santa?" Lauren asked. "He's an institution at Community Hall." The six-foot tall Santa had been an icon there since Lauren was a little girl.

"Barbara promised she'd have him as good as new in no time."

Relieved, Lauren adjusted her handbag on her shoulder. "Has anyone suggested Baxter might be better off at home instead of in the middle of things?"

"I did, but he's hosting the Critter Christmas Parade, so Barbara insists he be there."

"Translation, he'll destroy the place while they're gone."

"That's my guess."

The parade. "You did limit the costume entrants in the parade to dogs and cats, right?"

"I did," he assured her. "I heard all the stories about the raccoons, goats, and the skunk."

"Oh, good." Lauren laughed and David joined her. It seemed so odd, strange, to laugh with him, especially still not knowing why he'd broken their engagement.

She didn't want to laugh with him, or to notice the little changes in him, and she really didn't want him to appeal to her as much as he always had. She took a step back, sobered. "Carter is waiting."

They walked deeper into the printing shop and approached the counter.

Carter, in his late fifties, stood on the other side of it. "Glad you two could finally make it. Where's the design?"

"What design?" David asked, glancing at Lauren.

"For the tickets," Carter said.

"I don't have a design, Carter," Lauren told him. "Can't you just do what you did last year?"

"I could, but your mother won't like it," he said. "I'm not the artist she is but let me see what I can do. Give me fifteen minutes or so."

"Okay," David said. "We'll step over to Granny's and grab a cup of coffee."

"Fine." Carter shouted back at them and disappeared into the back of his shop.

"That's probably not a good idea," Lauren told David. "Us going to Granny's."

"Why not?"

Let him find out for himself. She'd dealt with all of it for months before leaving for Atlanta. "Never mind."

They walked two doors down and into Granny's. It wasn't meal time—too late for lunch, too early for dinner—but the men's afternoon coffee club was there, and a smattering of tables were filled with women who'd teamed up for last minute shopping.

Ignoring the sudden silence and the stares, she and David sat down across from each other at a table near the window—their second mistake, in Lauren's opinion—and ordered coffee. David asked for a slice of apple pie, and asked Lauren if she'd like one. "No, thanks," she said.

Two minutes later, the first sidewalk gawkers stopped at the window to stare at them, then came inside and sat down at a table nearby. More followed.

The waitress refilled their cups. "You two are good for business."

Lauren knew exactly what she meant.

David appeared baffled, and uttered, "What?"

"Nothing," the waitress said. "Enjoy your pie."

He looked to Lauren to explain.

She plastered on a smile. "They're curious about us."

"Who?"

"The people filling up the place." How could he not have noticed the stares? The covert glimpses. The bold watches.

"What are they expecting?"

"For us to argue or make a scene. The romantics likely are hoping we'll make up." It felt good to say it all aloud. To lay it out there, and for him to grasp what she'd dealt with all that time.

"You're kidding, right?"

She slid him her best deadpan expression. "Do I look like I'm kidding?"

"You're smiling, but it isn't touching your eyes. Not kidding." He turned solemn. "So, what do we do?"

"Nothing."

"At all?"

"At all." She shrugged. "You put on your innocent face, bury your feelings, and just do what you do." At least, until you just couldn't do it anymore. Then, you left, hoping to find peace, and eventually discovering peace is elusive and nowhere to be found.

He stilled. "You're speaking from experience."

"I am."

"Is this what happened to you after…?"

"Innocent face." She smiled again. More plastic even than the last one. No way was she discussing this further with him under these watchful eyes. "Let's talk about what's next on the plans, shall we?"

"The photographer," David said, then polished off the last bite of his pie.

"Binks?"

He nodded. "She can meet us at 4:00, if we're done with Carter by then. If not, tomorrow morning at 8:00." He dabbed at his mouth with his napkin. "Short meeting. Just to touch base and make sure she knows what we want."

Lauren checked her watch. "We'd best get back over to Carter's then."

"Great."

As they neared the door, the quiet at Granny's erupted into chatter. Lauren had expected it. David had not. "Keep walking," she told him. "Don't look back."

Outside, he stepped to her side. "Why are they doing that?"

"Because this is a small, tight-knit community and, in those, that's what people do."

He paused outside the door to Carter's. "Why do they care?"

"Because they do. You've been here two years, David. You should know the community is like a big family. Everyone feels totally justified to have opinions on everyone else's life. It's just one of those things. Like breathing."

"That's not been my experience," he said. "People here were a little on the frosty side. Especially at first."

"Good." Shameful, but she was glad to hear it. Shame rippled through her. "Sorry. Seriously, I am sorry. I've seen that side. I didn't like it either."

"I expected a cool reception," he said, leaning heavily on his cane. "But not freezing."

Is that why her mother had stepped in to help him gain acceptance? That sense of betrayal reared up inside Lauren. She shoved it back down, buried it. "Well, that appears to be behind you now."

"It was, or I thought it was."

"Until I came home."

"Yes," he confessed. "But I've been expecting you to come back for a long time."

He thought she'd stayed away because he was here. He didn't know she had been kept in the dark about his moving to Holt Ridge. "Couldn't avoid it forever. For better or worse, my family is here. These are my people."

"It's home." He opened the door to Carter's print shop.

She drew in an exaggerated breath. "Exactly. It's home."

Inside, Carter had a mock-up waiting for them. He turned it around on the front counter. "Will this do?"

The ticket wasn't just serviceable. It had her mother's artistic flair. "Did Mom do this?"

"I've been printing the dinner and dance tickets for your mother for a long time," Carter said. "I know what she likes."

In the lower right corner were tiny initials. VH. Vanessa Holt. "She did this one?"

Carter avoided Lauren's eyes. "It's a hybrid of some ideas she had. I wanted to stay true to her style. It's very distinct." He lifted a shoulder. "With her being sick and all, I didn't want her disappointed, so I've been working at this to do a ticket she'd like."

He wanted her mother's approval. "Well, I think she would be very pleased, Carter. You did a great job."

He smiled, transforming his stern face. "Thank you, Lauren."

"Great." David tapped the floor with his cane. "Print them up, Carter. When can we pick them up? I hate to rush you, but we've got to get them to the business owners so they can sell them, and we're running out of time."

"First thing in the morning." Carter leaned against the counter. "I'll get them printed and cut tonight."

"Thank you," Lauren said. "Sorry you're having to put in overtime."

"Anything for your mom." He smiled. "She's always been there for my family and me."

She had been for everyone on the Ridge. It was her duty as a Holt. Until Atlanta, Carter would have said the same thing of Lauren. But not anymore. Now, she was the outsider who had abandoned them. They didn't see how they'd driven her to it. Truthfully, they'd probably be mortified if they knew it.

"You can pick them up anytime after 8:00." Carter put the papers back in his file.

"Wonderful." Lauren smiled. "Thanks again."

David nodded and they walked outside, paused on the

sidewalk and he checked his watch. "We can make it to the photographer, if you're up for it."

"I am." Lauren admitted. "I'll feel better when some of these items are ticked off the list."

"So will I." He looked across the circle to B & F Photography. "I'm glad your mom stuck with the locals."

"It'd take a natural disaster or a blast to get her to use any business not in Holt Ridge." Lauren fell into step beside him. "I notice your limp is getting worse as the day wears on. Does it hurt?"

He nodded to a woman pushing a stroller down the sidewalk. "Afternoon, Jamie. How's Grant?"

"Fine, thanks, David." The young mother smiled and walked on. "Good to have you home, Lauren."

"Thanks." She forced herself to smile. Jamie had been especially thoughtless in her comments about David's defection. Seems she'd forgotten all that now, but Lauren hadn't. Still, it didn't serve anyone well to be ungracious about it.

At the corner, they crossed the street. The concrete was wet and bits of ice were forming. "Careful," Lauren said. "Sidewalk is refreezing."

He slid a bit, and Lauren grabbed his arm. "Hold on."

"Thanks." He grabbed her arm. "The patches of ice make walking tricky."

"For me, too." If he resented her help, he didn't show it. Actually, he seemed less uncomfortable. "So," they walked on, "does it hurt?"

"A bit, but it's not bad. The ice is not my friend."

"Then why did you move here? I mean, where it snows so much?" Clumsily put, but it was a fair question.

He looked away. "When we were…you know, I came to think of Holt Ridge as home." He shrugged. "I have no roots or family. That sense of belonging appealed."

"It's nice to belong, isn't it?" A couple stood center circle on the snow-covered green looking at the memorial for the men and women from here who had served in the military. Above it, flew the flag, stiff in the brisk wind. At its base sat a large pot of bright red poinsettias.

"It is nice to belong," he said. "Especially since I know you haven't stayed away because I was here." David glanced over at her, their arms still looped. "I worried about that, but your mother assured me my presence wouldn't make a difference to you."

Her mother was wrong, not that Lauren would admit it to another breathing soul. He'd left her and ended up with her family, her friends and neighbors, and her place here. She'd ended up with an apartment in a city of strangers and a job teaching kids she didn't know. Maybe she should be more adult about it, but the truth was, she'd lost or forfeited everything, and she still didn't understand why. The question burned on her tongue, and she opened her mouth to ask it.

"Finally, we're here." David reached for the door to B & F Photography and then opened it wide.

Whether deliberate avoidance or just bad timing, the window of opportunity for her questions had closed.

A woman about forty wearing a Santa hat and red sneakers stood at the counter and smiled. "Lauren Holt. As I live and breathe." She rushed over and hugged Lauren. "Gosh, it's good to see you, girl."

"Hi, Binks." Lauren hugged her back, then stepped away. "How are you?"

"Mad as fire that you ran off and forgot about us," she said in a burst that held no heat. "But you're home now, so all's forgiven." Binks turned to glance at David. "Hey. How's the leg?"

"Okay."

"You doing your PT like you're supposed to?"

He was doing physical therapy. Lauren went silent and observed.

"I don't dare not to. Everyone on the Ridge reports the least little infraction straight to Dr. Fleming."

Binks laughed. "Got to keep you on the straight and narrow." She pointed to a grouping of two chairs and a small sofa. "Let's sit and go over the checklist."

"You have a checklist?" Lauren asked, more relieved than she wanted to acknowledge.

David nearly choked.

Binks' expression went blank, then she quickly covered it. "Um, last year's. Your mom has so many traditions in the events, not much changes year to year."

David looked relieved, and Lauren wondered why. He probably feared they'd have to hash out what they wanted covered and was relieved that a lot had already been done, just not on paper.

Binks took a chair. Lauren sat on the sofa, expecting David to sit in the second chair. He chose to sit beside her instead, which had Binks hiding a half-smile. "So, we'll start with the sleigh rides and bonfire. We always grab photos of those," Binks said. "The Popes have been explicit on what they want—Baxter is hosting the Critters Christmas Parade. I'm telling you right now, if Jonas Calder brings a skunk this year, I'm quitting," Binks warned.

David piped in. "The critter parade is limited to cats and dogs—and a turtle. Jamie's little boy has a pet turtle. I didn't think Vanessa would want him shut out of the parade, so I waived the cat-or-dog requirement for him."

"Good thing," Binks said, turning to Lauren. "His daddy rescued a tiger. Grant would have entered it, and tigers are cats."

"Dodged a bullet on that one." Lauren turned to David. "How many waivers have you issued?"

He twisted his mouth. "Just a couple." Intentionally evasive, he parked his cane at his side and told Binks. "Don't worry. Nothing that will send you running."

"Glad to hear it." She scanned the list. "Now if Baxter just behaves, we'll be good to go."

The odds of that mischief-maker staying in line were slim to none. But if he was as cute as he typically was when misbehaving, his transgressions would be endured, and he would be forgiven.

"I'm sure he'll be fine," Binks said. "But Barbara has been worried lately."

"Why?" Lauren asked.

Binks didn't answer, so Lauren looked at David.

He lifted a hand. "She and Kenneth are concerned that Baxter has been depressed. That's why they're taking him with them everywhere all the time. They don't want him alone, and they want to keep him busy."

"Depressed?" He hadn't seemed depressed. Spoiled rotten, yes, but not depressed.

"And anxious," Binks said, coming to the dog's defense. "He has been a little jumpy."

"When?" Lauren swiped at her slacks.

"Outside Community Hall," Binks said. "He chewed up a couple little sprigs of holly, and Jessica Weaver was not at all happy about it. She fussed at him. Poor Baxter looked ready for a breakdown." Binks shook her head. "Barbara nearly never got him or Jessica calmed down."

Spoiled rotten. That rascal had everyone wrapped around his paw.

"That leaves the Christmas dinner and dance. It's still a dinner and dance, right?" Binks asked.

"Every year for nearly thirty years," Lauren said. "No way am I brave enough to break that tradition."

"Typically, I try to get candid shots of everyone, but I was thinking this year, we should get family shots, too." Binks seemed a little shy. "The Historical Society was complaining that all its photos are older and some of the new families aren't included. That's not sitting well with them."

"Family photos sounds like a great idea, Binks." Lauren looked to David, who nodded his agreement.

"Awesome." Binks smiled and closed her file. "That's it then, we're done."

"Almost," David said. "Will the Historical Society assist on the sitting fees?"

Binks grinned. "They're covering the entire dinner and dance event and the family photos."

"All of it?" That surprised David. "Great."

"Gets even better." Binks wrinkled her nose. "They're paying for half of the Christmas parade. The Chamber of Commerce is donating the other half, and half on the bonfire."

"Binks, that's amazing." David gave Binks a high five. "Well done."

"I thought so." She laughed. "Bailey Adams and Paul's folks are covering the sleigh rides."

"Paul's folks?" Lauren cocked her head.

"Tom's Hardware." Binks flushed. "Paul helps me on a lot on photo shoots."

"Full disclosure," David said, teasing Binks. "They're an item."

"Wonderful." Lauren tried not to envy the little leap of heart so evident on Binks' face. The look of a young woman in love.

"Binks, you've outdone yourself. Vanessa will be thrilled." David reached for his cane.

"She's the reason they've been so eager to help out," Binks said. "You know everyone around here loves Miss Vanessa."

They did. Her mother cast a long shadow, and always had. "She'll be ecstatic, Binks. Thank you."

"Sure thing. I hope it perks her up and she beats that nasty infection." Binks walked them to the door. "You tell her we're all pulling for her."

"I will." Lauren smiled, praying that would be just what her mother needed to hear to fight hard and recover.

Outside, David turned to Lauren. "Any word from the hospital?"

"Not since early this morning. The antibiotics hadn't kicked in then, and Jessica warned me Mom could go either way."

Worry crept over his face. "You should be there with her."

"Caroline's there. I was given orders to get the events planned and to make sure every event goes off without a hitch."

David grunted. "That's asking for a lot with all these events. What goes off without a hitch?"

"Nothing." Lauren looked at him, and shrugged. "Every event has hiccups. Some are little, others are not." The memory of informing everyone the wedding was off. The surprise and shock and gasps. Even by phone, it had been horrible—and partially her fault for not putting out word immediately on receiving his text. A part of her had refused to believe the breakup wasn't a terrible joke. Surely, he'd change his mind. But it wasn't, and he didn't. Finally, she'd accepted there wasn't going to be further word from him and she, her mother and Caroline had contacted everyone the next morning. At least, Lauren had not been left standing alone at the altar in her wedding gown. Being spared that humiliation was a small mercy.

"I guess I left you with a mess, cancelling the wedding the night before." David spoke softly. "I'm sorry, Lauren."

"One day, I'm going to ask you why you did that." She warned him.

"But not today?"

"No, not today." She checked her watch. "I want to know, but I need to get to the hospital and see about my mother."

"Can we use that appointment in the morning to meet with Barbara Pope about the flowers?"

The backup appointment with Binks, in case they weren't done at Carter's in time today. "Eight o'clock, right?"

"Yes." He stopped at the corner. "I'm parked down here. You need a lift?"

"No, I'm parked around the circle." She pointed in the opposite direction. "Eight works fine. I'll meet you there."

"Okay." He smiled that smile. "It was good being with you today, Lauren."

It was agony. Reminding her of all that once was and wasn't anymore. But it was good, too, in those moments she'd forgotten to be furious with him for tossing something so special away as if it had meant nothing. "Have a good evening, David." She turned and walked away, crossed the street, then down the circle to the far corner. When she rounded it and dropped out of sight, she took a deep breath and relaxed.

David stood where she'd left him, watching her go.

Jamie paused beside him on the sidewalk. The baby shook a rattle inside the stroller. "David Decker, what are you doing? You still haven't told her."

Jamie's disapproval came through loud and clear. "Not yet."

Shaking her head, Jamie frowned. "David, just tell her."

"When it's time, I will," he said. "And you better not say a word before then, Jamie."

"I won't. No one will." Jamie's frown deepened. "But don't you think it's time? It's been—"

"When it's time, I'll know it," he said, interrupting her. "It's not yet. That much I know for fact."

"You underestimated her before," Jamie said. "Don't do it again." Jamie walked on, pushing the stroller, making her way down the circle.

David walked down to his car. Had he underestimated Lauren? He didn't think he had, but he wasn't without doubt. Jamie could be right. Maybe it was time? But Lauren and he had been getting along so well. He hated to risk losing that.

He unlocked the car, got inside, then closed the door. Stretching over, he put his cane on the passenger's floorboard, met his eyes in the rearview mirror and whispered out loud the words he feared most. "From all signs, buddy, it won't make much difference. I'm afraid your time has come and gone."

7

December 20th
5:15 PM

"JESSICA." Lauren spotted her near the nurse's station. "How's mom?"

"About the same." Jessica frowned. "I don't know, Lauren. It's almost as if she doesn't want to fight, which is counter to everything we both know about your mother."

"She said she'd decided to—fight, I mean." Lauren hooked her handbag on her shoulder. "Is she eating?"

"She is. But her fever breaks and comes back, breaks and comes back—not that it's unusual, but the antibiotics really should be working now…"

"And they're not." Lauren looked into her best friend's eyes. "Is she going to…" Lauren couldn't make herself say the word.

Jessica grabbed her hand, squeezed. "If she'd really

fight, it'd help. It just does. I've seen it a thousand times. This is just strange."

"What is?"

"It's as if something has broken her will." Jessica's brown eyes widened. "That is the last thing I'd ever expect from your mother."

"Me, too." It was an alien concept. Her mother had always had an iron will.

A bell chirped, then chirped again. "That's Rory, again. He's having a love affair with his call button. I'd better get down there," Jessica said. "If I don't answer right away, he slides right past his usual grumpy state into roar." She smiled. "I'll stop by your mom's when I can."

Lauren went into her mother's room, washed her hands, and spotted a note from Caroline on the bedside tray. "Gone home. Had all the people time I can take for one day. Mom is doing better, despite what Dr. Fleming says. I saw him this morning, and he says she's stable."

Her mother stirred awake. "Lauren."

"Hi, Mom." She planted a kiss to her forehead. It was cool.

"So how did the planning go today?"

"First things first," Lauren said, pulling the chair closer to the bed. "Has something upset you recently?"

"No."

"Then your spirit isn't broken?" Again, she was grateful they'd always been blunt.

"Lauren, don't be silly. That's so unlike you."

"I'm not being silly. I'm serious."

"What is this all about?"

Lauren grasped her mother's hand. "We've always been honest with each other, so I'm just going to spit this out." When her mother nodded, Lauren went on. "The medical staff doesn't understand why the antibiotics haven't started working. That's becoming a challenge for you."

"They're working. I can feel it," her mother said. "I'm improving, Lauren."

"I pray you are. But it's not showing up in your numbers yet."

"Dr. Fleming says I'm stable. Tell Jessica to quit worrying about me and my spirit. We're both intact and I'm going to be fine."

"Promise?" Lauren blinked hard. "Mom, you know I love you, right?"

"Of course. And you know I love you."

"Then tell me the truth."

Her mother's face flushed. "About what?"

That surprised Lauren. "Is there more than one truth you're withholding from me?"

"Did you come here just to pick a fight with me?" Vanessa Holt sniffed. "Don't make me prefer to watch Caroline read over a visit with you."

She had a point. Still… "Point taken. But if something were bothering you, you would tell me, right?"

"I would." Her mother nodded. "Now, enough about all that. Tell me how the plans are coming along."

She didn't want to discuss herself or her condition, and if Vanessa Holt made up her mind to not discuss something, wild horses or a tow truck couldn't drag anything out of her. Lauren gave in to the subject shift graciously. "It was a good day. The tickets are being printed as we speak. Carter will have them ready in the morning."

"Did you see Binks?"

"I did. You're going to be happy with her report."

"I am?"

Lauren nodded. "The Historical Society is paying the sitting fees, and Binks is doing family photos. The

Chamber and Tom's Hardware are splitting some of the other events costs. If the dinner and dance sales pick up, then it looks like we're set for a profitable fundraiser." Lauren touched her mother's hand. "I have an idea on that. A website. I'm hoping it'll do the trick."

"I sure hope so. You know how much your father loved music."

So that's the reason she'd been so dedicated to the festivity projects all these years. "He did."

Her mother gazed at the wall, seeing something far beyond it. "He wasn't always that way. About music, I mean. When we went to our first Christmas dinner and dance, he became a diehard fan."

"Really?" Lauren hadn't known that.

"Really." Her mother smiled. "That night, I told him I loved him, and I knew he loved me, and it was high time we got married."

Lauren gasped and laughed. "You proposed to Dad?"

"If I hadn't, we'd still be dating, and you and Caroline wouldn't be here." She laughed. "He was stunned, but he accepted." Her mom's smile lingered, curving her lips. "He said he had intended to ask me that night—he had the ring and everything—but he was too nervous to talk, so he kept postponing. I think my impatience puffed him up a little. He accepted right away."

Lauren laughed. "I can't imagine Dad nervous."

"I was terrified, too."

"No, you were determined. You get something in your head and that's that. You've always known exactly what you wanted."

"I have. Most of the time." Her mother's voice weakened. "Honestly, David really shook my confidence."

"Let's don't discuss him. Let's discuss happy times and you."

Her mother ignored her. "I just knew he was the one for you."

Clearly, she intended they discuss him anyway. "You weren't exactly crazy about him."

"Nonsense. I have always been crazy about him," she countered. "He loved you above all else. I saw it in everything he said and did. What mother wouldn't love that?"

But he'd left her, and while she had trouble remembering sometimes when they were together, he didn't love her anymore. Lauren sobered. "Can we not talk about David? Please." It couldn't be good for her mother, and it definitely wasn't good for Lauren.

"Indulge me a moment. Just a moment." She persisted. "Did you two get along well today?"

"It was fine. We've got so much to do and so little time. The intense focus on the plans keeps either of us from thinking about much else. That's a good thing."

"So much to do?" Her mother looked confused.

"The printer, the photographer, the florist, caterer, then the events."

Her mother looked a little lost. "Don't forget the favors. They have to be made."

"What are they?"

"Ribbon-wrapped candy canes for Santa to give to the children."

"Santa?"

Her mother's eyes stretched wide. "Don't tell me David forgot Santa."

"I'm sure he hasn't," Lauren reassured her mother. "We just haven't yet discussed it."

"Well, you two better get busy." Worry etched her face and settled in her eyes. "We have the Holt reputation to consider, and we don't want anyone disappointed."

"Believe me, we are trying hard to do everything exactly as you would want it done."

"I'm sure you are, dear."

"Seems everyone is going the extra mile this year."

"I'm glad to hear that."

"They're doing it for you, Mom. You think people don't notice all you do, but they do notice, and it means a lot to them."

"What I do is a privilege, Lauren." She closed her eyes. "I'm sorry. I'm so tired. I need to rest a little while."

"Of course." Lauren patted her mother's arm, and stood up. "I'll go get busy on those favors."

"The candy canes and ribbons are in my She Shack."

The little backyard building that had been her mother's art studio and sanctuary and hobby room all Lauren's life had always been called her studio. But after Dad's death, Mom recalled once he had referred to it as her She Shack, and the name had stuck. "Mom, can I ask you a question?"

"Yes." She sounded groggy.

"Why did you help David? When everyone here was freezing him out, he said you helped him. Why did you do that?"

"Because you loved him, Lauren."

"But he broke my heart."

"Yes, he did."

"I don't understand."

"Think on it for a while." She closed her eyes and fell asleep.

The conversation wasn't what she'd hoped for, but it was all she was going to get. Walking out with as many questions as when she'd walked in, Lauren rounded the corner and saw Jessica.

"I'm having to pull a double. One of the nurses called

in sick, so no Granny's at seven for me tonight. Sorry, Lauren."

"It's just as well," Lauren said. "I was just informed we have to make favors for Santa to give to the kids. Nothing fancy. Just ribbons on candy canes."

"Before you go, let's grab a quick bite in the cafeteria. I'm starving."

"Okay."

When they'd gotten their food and sat down to eat, Jessica scooped up a French fry and dragged it through sour cream. She'd always done that. Had never been a ketchup fan. "Reverend Wong's got a group meeting tonight at the church. I'll bet if you ask, they'll put the favors together for you."

"Great idea." Lauren spread her napkin in her lap. "We have it all. When I leave here, I'll drop by and ask."

Halfway through her salad, Jessica got that look in her eye. "What?" Lauren asked.

"I promised myself I'd wait for you to bring him up, but it's clear that's not going to happen, and I'm dying to know, so I give up. How did it go with David today?"

Lauren took a sip of tea before she answered. "Honestly?"

"Always."

"It was hard. I've been on an emotional rollercoaster all day."

"Because…?"

"He's being nice. And acting like nothing happened." She shrugged. "Every other word brought back a memory, and most of them were good, which really knocked me for a loop."

"I can imagine."

"At first, I was annoyed because he was here."

"I figured." Jessica harrumphed. "I would be furious.

It's almost like he stepped into your life here, and you're stuck in Georgia."

"Exactly."

Jessica nodded. "The first six months he was here, that's all I thought about every time I saw him, which was often."

Surprised, Lauren asked, "Why?"

"It's a small town, Lauren." Jessica shrugged. "Impossible to avoid anyone for long."

"True, and that's exactly how him being here struck me." Lauren sighed. "I felt betrayed by everyone—even Mom, for accepting him, and that's just wrong. I shouldn't feel that way, Jess."

"I don't know a woman who wouldn't feel that way—at least, at first. It had to be a shock."

"It was."

"All this time, and your mom never said a word about him being here?"

"Not one. Caroline either," Lauren added, "or you."

"I thought you knew, and you'd bring it up when you were ready."

Oddly, that made Lauren feel better.

"So today was hard. It stirred up a lot of old feelings. But you got through it."

"It'd be better if I always remembered they were old feelings. Not current ones. It's easy to forget sometimes."

"Give yourself a break. You loved him, and you thought you'd love him forever."

"I did." Lauren dragged a thumb down her sweating glass. "It wasn't all bad. The memory rushes aside. Well, many of those were good, too," she admitted. "Actually, it was kind of nice to talk to him or to remember some little something and for the first question in my mind not to be, 'Why?'"

"Maybe it's time for you to just ask him why. Put it to bed."

"I almost have a couple times. But something always comes up that he's in a rush to handle."

"He's avoiding the subject?"

"I believe he is. But he did try to open a discussion door once today. The timing was bad, though. I had to get over here to see Mom. Caroline was supposed to see Dr. Fleming on rounds and give me a report. I had hoped she'd still be here, but she left a note. You know how she maxes out on people."

"She left just before eleven," Jessica said. "Frankly, I'm shocked she made it that long." Jessica took a bite of fry. "Probably wouldn't have if Rory hadn't been here, too."

"He does have a calming effect on her."

"Things will get better, Lauren." Jessica finished her fries. "People will stop gawking and gossiping and you'll get used to being around him. Things will get better."

"They didn't get better before."

"It hadn't been long enough since the wedding." Jessica waved a fingertip. "You know what I mean. This time is different."

"How?" It was still David and her.

"Once people realize you aren't going to kill each other or reunite in Town Circle, they'll get used to seeing you together and all this Christmas bustle will end, and then things will settle down."

"And I'll be back in Atlanta and he'll be here, living my life."

"Only if that's what you choose." Jessica looked her in the eye. "You control your life, my friend. Whether you stay or go back, that's up to you."

A smiling Jason joined them. "Ladies."

"You look particularly happy," Jessica said. "What's got that smile on your face?"

"I just heard Baxter dug a hole near the steps at Community Hall yesterday. Before anyone could fill it in, Santa Number Two, Rory, took a nose dive into it. Heard he was taken to the E.R. and wanted to check on him."

"He was admitted," Jessica said. "My floor."

"Oh, no." Lauren grimaced. *Santa Number Two* registered. "Is he okay?"

"Sandra Mason says he's fine," Jason said. "Well, he might have a sprained ankle, but that's a good thing."

"How can a sprained ankle be a good thing?" Jessica dabbed at her mouth with her napkin.

Jason grinned. "Baxter can outrun him."

Lauren chuckled. "He's on the bad dog list, eh?"

"Oh, yeah. Santa Number Two is not happy. Tom said he griped all the way over here about getting the mayor to issue a proclamation that the Popes had to keep Baxter at home."

Lauren frowned. "Seriously?"

Jason nodded.

"That is not going to happen," Jessica insisted. "Baxter has been depressed."

"And anxious." Lauren added.

"I've heard that, too." Jason folded his hands together. "I reminded Rory about Janelle, and how rescuing Baxter had pulled the Popes back from the brink after she passed away. He's just raising Cain. He's not going to do anything."

"Barbara and Kenneth will be happy to hear it."

"They would have fought him tooth and nail and demanded a "Save Baxter" vote be put on the ballot." Jessica said.

"Wouldn't that be a mess? Santa versus Baxter? The

kids would be really upset." Lauren said. "Who was Santa One this year?"

"Nick. He's always Santa One."

"Where's he?"

"Up on the third floor in isolation. He has the flu."

"Hate to hear that," Lauren said. "So, Rory was filling in for Nick, and now he's in the hospital, too?"

Jessica nodded. "He's been giving us fits up on the floor."

Lauren winced, recalled the call button affair remark from earlier. "If they're both out of commission, then we've got a problem." This was not good. Two Santas down. Who could they get to fill in at this late date? "Does David know?"

"I assume everyone in the county knows by now," Jason said.

Rory was just cantankerous enough to file a complaint, too. "Santa versus Baxter," Lauren grunted. "The kids will be outraged and confused."

"The adults, too." Jessica chimed in. "Barbara and Kenneth might spoil the mutt but who can stay mad at Baxter? He's charming."

"He's a pain," Jason shared his opinion, "but everyone loves him anyway."

"Endearing, my mother says." Lauren stood up. "I've got to touch base with David on this, and then go talk to Reverend Wong. Wish me luck. Otherwise, it's going to be a long night." Lauren lifted her tray. "Let me know if there's any change on mom, Jess."

"I will. Don't worry. I've got her."

"Thanks."

Jason watched Lauren go. "She doesn't know about David, does she?"

"Not yet." Jessica sighed.

"He should tell her."

"Considering the internal war she's got raging inside her right now, I agree." Jessica took a drink from her cup. "Maybe that's why he's waiting. Letting her get used to him being around first."

"Honey, that woman is never going to get used to him being around. Not when she doesn't have a clue what all this is about."

"She feels invaded and betrayed," Jessica told him. "But I think she also still has strong feelings for him."

"That should make it easier…or harder," Jason said. "I can see it both ways."

"So can I." Jessica lifted her hands. "Guess we'll have to wait and see how it all works out."

Jason sent her a warning look. "Either way, she's going to be really ticked you didn't tell her, Jess. You know that, right?"

"I do." Her expression turned solemn. "But I can't tell her. If I did and she walked away, I'd never forgive myself. Every day, I'd wonder if I just stayed out of it, things would have a better ending."

"I hear you." He clasped her hand atop the table. "But she's still going to be really ticked off at you. Just be prepared so you don't get hurt."

"Yes, she will. She'll be the one hurt. I hate that, but I'll just have to deal with it."

Becky Grayson stopped by Jessica's table, carrying her food tray. "I don't know what's put such a sour look on your face, but I know something that will put a smile on that mouth."

Jessica looked up at Mrs. Grayson. "What's that?" She could use a smile. The idea of Lauren being hurt by Jessica's silence did not sit well on her shoulders, and it sat even heavier on her heart.

Becky Grayson smiled. "Tom just came in to pick up Rory Hardin. He's been discharged."

Hope lit up inside Jessica. "Seriously?"

Becky nodded.

Jason seemed confused. "Tell me again how Rory Hardin connects around here. I should recall more, but I don't see him much."

"Rory's a recluse no one sees much. He's related to Tom and Sylvia Miller—the Hardware Store. Rory is Tom's grumpy old uncle."

"He looks like Santa," Jason said. "Long white beard."

"Except for the scowl," Jessica said. "He's been like a bear with a thorn in his paw since he got here," she said. "I guess it's not really his fault. He's used to peace and quiet. All the people and noise are making him more grumpy than usual. Thank goodness Caroline rescued us for a while."

"There's the smile," Becky said, then walked on and joined two other nurses at a nearby table.

"The only person Rory Hardin has ever liked is Caroline Holt. Those two spend hours and hours together and never say a word."

"Odd," Jason said. "Two recluses hanging out together like that."

"Caroline was really close to her dad. So was Rory. I think they spend time together to remember him—but that's just a guess, since neither ever says enough for you know what's on their minds."

"Other than grumping about the people and noise in here."

"He does do that." Jessica nodded. "But Caroline was here yesterday and some this morning, which gave us a welcome respite."

"Not surprising she was here." Jason sipped from his

coffee cup. "Lauren was doing her mom's planning and Vanessa is awfully sick. They have to be worried."

"I expect they're terrified of losing her," Jessica agreed. "But Caroline spent most of the time sitting with Rory. Don't get me wrong. We were glad to see it. He didn't push his call button once the entire time she was here."

"Maybe he didn't need attention because he had attention," Jason said. "Maybe Caroline knew the staff needed a break."

Jessica thought that over. "Could be. Or it could be she is terrified of losing her mom like she did her dad. Rory gives Caroline strength. Always has. That much I do know."

"Her father-figure?"

"I think so." Jessica covered Jason's hand on the table with her own. "I've got to get back to work."

8

December 20th
6:00 PM

LAUREN WALKED into her mother's She Shack, and immediately felt her mother's presence. She looked to the little reading nook where she'd watched her mother sit and dream through the front window for years.

No one disturbed her when she was in here. Dad had laid down that rule early on, not that it wasn't just known. Both Lauren and Caroline had sensed that when her mother came here, it was for solitude or to think. They just didn't intrude.

All the little touches were feminine like the woman, and on the little fireplace mantel she had photos of the family going back to the War Between the States. Dad's ancestors and her own. Photos of Lauren and Jessica at play, and one of Caroline sitting in the woods, her back to the base of a tree, her nose in a book. Lauren smiled. Her mother knew her daughters well. And this daughter squeezed her eyes shut and prayed hard her mother was improving and she recovered. Lauren couldn't imagine life without her at the helm.

And she would never forgive herself for isolating herself, wasting three years of living without seeing her.

"What are you doing in here?" Caroline stood at the doorway, frowning.

Lauren jerked. "You scared me. I didn't know you were at home."

"I left you a note at the hospital."

"I got it." Lauren scanned the She Shack for the candy canes and spotted them beside the work table. The reels of ribbon were stacked on top.

Staying at the door, Caroline folded her arms. "So, what are you doing in Mom's She Shack?"

"She told me the favors for the kids from Santa haven't been done either. The supplies are in here." Lauren moved to the stack. "I stopped by the church earlier and Reverend Wong has a group meeting tonight. He says they'll put the favors together. I've got to take the candy canes and ribbons to them." She checked her watch. "And I need to hurry. They'll be there in thirty minutes."

"I'll help you put them in the car."

A thousand packages of canes and all the spools of ribbon would take several trips. "Thanks."

Caroline shrugged. "If she'd told me, I could have done these for her." She grabbed a stack of canes. "Of course, she probably figured I'd mess them up."

Lauren grabbed a stack. "She knows you don't like this kind of stuff. That's more likely why she didn't ask." When doubt flashed across Caroline's face, Lauren added, "You have cultivated that opinion because you don't like mixing on social events."

"I could have done this at home, though." Caroline shrugged. "It's different."

They walked to the car, and Caroline packed the trunk while Lauren returned to the She Shack to get more canes.

When she bent to lift packages from the stack, her elbow scraped a small stack of papers. They slid off the edge of the table and fluttered to the floor.

She bent to pick them up—and saw they were pages of plans that should have been in her mother's packet in her dad's office file. The ticket sample, which looked amazingly similar to the one Carter created. She looked closer. Exactly the same, actually. The agreement with Binks and the flower order, the caterer order with Kenneth Pope. Everything had been planned and done. So why were she and David having to do it all again?

Her mother. Forcing them to spend time together. Matchmaking.

Betrayed all over again, Lauren stuffed the pages into her coat pocket, grabbed the final stack of canes and the last box of spools of ribbon, then rushed to the car, where Caroline stood waiting. "Hurry, Caroline. I'm going to be late."

She wiggled her fingers. "Hand them over. I can't put them in until I get them."

Lauren passed the bunch to her sister. Soon she was seated in her mother's car.

Caroline shut the trunk. "Are you coming back after you drop all this off?"

"I have to stop by the hospital first. Mom went to sleep right after I arrived, so I haven't really talked to her today."

"She goes to sleep to avoid being asked questions." Caroline stepped back, away from the car. "If you want her to stay awake, don't ask her anything she doesn't want to answer."

She'd done exactly that. "Jessica said it was the medicine. It makes them sleep to heal. All their energy is going to fight the infection when they're sleeping."

"True, from what I've read. But Mom's falling asleep at the most convenient times. Every time I brought up you or David with all this planning, which has to be hard on you, she went lights out. Suddenly." Caroline twisted her lips. "I'm just saying."

After finding those papers, Lauren had a pretty good idea why her mother would want to avoid questions about throwing David and her together to plan events. "Thanks for the tip."

Nodding, Caroline turned and walked back to the house. Lauren backed out of the driveway and drove to the church. She needed to think. What was she going to do about what she'd found? Should she tell David? Confront her mother? All the others on the Ridge had to know, too. No wonder the meetings with Carter and Binks were going so smoothly. Events always had kinks, no matter how well planned. Except these.

Lauren could be done and not have to see David again except at the events…

Temptation appealed but fell to uncertainty and flooded her. "Is that what she wanted? To get through all this and return to Atlanta still not knowing why he'd broken their engagement?

9

December 20th
8:00 PM

AT THE DOOR to her mother's room, Lauren heard voices inside, and paused.

"Better than I expected, but..." A man's voice penetrated the door.

David's voice.

"But not as well as you hoped?" her mother asked.

"I'm not sure," he said. "She seems fine. Actually, at times it feels like it used to, but when I look into her eyes, I see the hurt and her questions. So far, I've avoided them."

"Her having questions shouldn't surprise you, David. She doesn't know why you left her. Lauren intended to marry you. She loved you. Of course, those questions prey on her mind."

"You think I should tell her. I know that. But then I'll never know if..."

"Eavesdropping? At your age?" Jessica whispered from behind Lauren.

Lauren turned abruptly. "Jessica. What is David doing here, talking to my mother?" She sure wasn't drifting off to sleep while talking to him.

"He comes twice a day. Has since she's been here." Jessica steered Lauren further away from the door. "Since he came home, they've gotten very close."

"Home? Close?" Lauren didn't know how to feel about that.

"She thinks of him as a son, Lauren. That's why everyone accepts him as one of our own." Jessica put a hand on Lauren's arm. "Surely that doesn't surprise you. He was almost her son."

"Almost. Until he ditched me…in a text message."

"Until then, yes." Jessica said without heat.

All the pain and devastation Lauren had felt on receiving and reading that message returned with force. "Does he have any idea how much that hurt? How hard it was to accept that he wasn't coming back and there'd be no wedding, no life together?" Lauren's voice cracked. "He broke my heart, Jess. Shattered it. And three years later, I still don't know why."

"Oh, wow." Jessica stilled. "You still love him."

Lauren avoided answering that directly. "I still care. I wish I could stop. I've tried, believe me. But I still wish for that—"

"David?"

"For the marriage I thought I'd have with the man I wanted."

"You haven't moved on."

"I can't." Lauren felt her eyes burn, tears well. "I thought I was gaining ground, dating James in Atlanta, but…"

"He's not David."

Lauren nodded he wasn't. "None of them are."

"And seeing David again brought all those old feelings back."

Lauren sniffed. "To be honest, I can't say they ever left." She sighed and stiffened. "I suspected it would always be that way, but when I saw him, I knew it would, and it's even worse." She looked away, waited for a woman in a walker to pass them in the hallway and step beyond earshot. "The thing is, even if I called the questions and he answered them, no matter what he said, I'd still be terrified that it wouldn't change anything."

"What do you mean?"

"He shut the book," she said. "But I'm stuck." She let Jessica see her upset. "I don't think this chapter of my life will ever close."

Jessica's mouth parted. "You'll love him forever."

A swell of fear had Lauren swallowing hard. "I will," she whispered. "I'll never forgive him, but I will always love him." She let out a grunt. "And doesn't that make me the biggest fool ever?"

Jessica hugged Lauren, spoke softly. "I think it makes you a lucky woman."

Lauren reared back. "Lucky? It's tragic."

"Not at all. You're a woman who knows exactly what she wants."

"A man who clearly never wanted me."

"Is he?" Jessica tilted her head. "Why is he here, then? In your home town? Courting your friends and family for acceptance?"

"I'd say to humiliate me, but that wouldn't be like him. Honestly, I don't know why." Lauren snapped back.

"Agreed. To humiliate is a lot of trouble for a man

wanting no more than that." Jessica patted her arm. "Has to be another reason. Maybe a good one."

"I know you're not suggesting I open myself up to be devastated again. Didn't he cost me enough the first time?"

"He did." Jessica nodded, lending weight to her words. "Opening up would take an enormous amount of courage, no doubt about it. But if you are going to love him forever, maybe it'd be worth taking the shot."

"I can't do that."

"You know best," Jessica said. "But, Lauren, do give yourself some time to think about it. Love is love. It can be as joyful and as merciless as any other emotion—and as relentless." Jessica gave her a goofy look and a soft smile. "It landed me a cowboy who wears boots and a hat and drives a truck—everything I've always said I never wanted." She laughed. "Don't tell me Fate doesn't have a sense of humor. I know better."

"Jason is a wonderful man, and he's totally crazy about you."

"He is." She adjusted the stethoscope hanging around her neck. "I'm going to marry him, but that's a secret."

"Ah, he doesn't know it yet." Lauren smiled.

"Not yet. But soon."

"The Christmas dinner and dance?"

She shrugged. "Maybe. I'm not sure yet." She was giving the idea time to settle in and take root.

"He's a lucky man."

"We both are." Jessica sighed. "I've got to get back to work. But first, promise me one thing."

"What?"

"Keep an open mind *and* an open heart." Jessica backed up a step. "I want to see my best friend happy. It's been such a long time, Lauren, and you deserve that chance."

Lauren nodded.

"Now go see your mom."

"But David is—"

"He left a few minutes ago."

"Jessica Weaver, you deliberately delayed me."

"Guilty," she admitted. "You were bent on confronting them about something, and I was bent on stopping you from making that mistake. You can be upset with me later. After you think things through. Now, go see your mom."

"Is she any better?"

"She's no worse, and that's a good sign. Dr. Fleming says it appears the infection is no longer spreading."

Stable. "That's great news."

"It is encouraging," Jessica said. "Maybe now she'll start healing. She was a little spunkier this afternoon, so something's lifted her spirits."

"Probably David's visits."

"Actually, I think she's thrilled her daughter is home."

"Maybe both."

"Maybe." Jessica's phone tinkled, and she stepped down the hallway to answer it.

One thing was certain, and, about it, Jessica had been right. Tonight wasn't the time to confront her mother about the plans she'd found in her She Shack. The infection was no longer spreading. Now she had the chance to actually heal.

Nothing was worth risking her progress. Not even long-missing answers to questions that haunted her daughter.

10

December 21st
8:00 AM

LAUREN WALKED into Barbara's Pope Floral with two minutes to spare, which was nothing short of a miracle, considering she'd tossed and turned all night, wondering what to do about this setup of her mother's. Another embarrassment she'd have to endure.

"Good morning." David passed her a cup of coffee. "You look like you could use this. Long night?"

"Extremely," she said. "The favors are handled, thanks to Reverend Wong and his group. I picked them up late last night."

"That's great. I picked up the tickets, so when we're done here, we can deliver them to the businesses on the Circle, if that's okay?"

"Fine." The sooner they got them out to the business

owners, the better. "We'll see if the marketing I've been doing online to nearby communities produces any results."

"Your mom told me about it. I've seen it on the Holt Ridge site and social media," he said. "That was a great idea."

"I should have told you, but considering it hasn't been done before, I didn't know if it would be effective, so I thought we'd just see. I absorbed the costs to sponsor the sub-domain and the ads."

"That's very generous of you."

"I don't want to disappoint my mother. This is important to her." Lauren craned her neck. "Where's Barbara?"

"In the back," he said with a nod toward the work area of the flower shop. "Baxter got into her roses and stomped a few poinsettias. She's checking to make sure he didn't get a thorn in his paw."

"He is one lucky pup." Lauren laughed. "Most people would be fussing at the dog."

"Not if they feared he was depressed and anxious."

"Especially if he helped them through grieving a lost child."

David smiled. "That, too. I think that's why people are so forgiving of whatever he does. Well, except for Santa. He's pretty miffed right now."

"Santa One or Santa Two?"

"Rory," David said. "The hole he stepped in that sprained his ankle. Turns out he has a hairline crack. He's been discharged, but he's going to be in one of those boots and on crutches for at least a month."

"I can see why he's not happy with Baxter," Lauren said. "So, what does this do for him playing Santa?" The last thing they needed was a mad dash hunt for Santa Three. "The parade is tomorrow."

"And the sleigh rides and the bonfire," David said. "Santa does all three events."

"And the dinner and dance."

"That, too." David dragged a hand through his hair. "After you called yesterday, I spoke to Reverend Wong. He will step in, if needed. But Rory insists he can cover the parade and the sleigh rides and bonfire, since he only has to sit and be present."

"I'm not sure that's a good idea." Lauren frowned. "The kids will be crawling all over him for photos." If one stepped on his foot and he started grousing, that wouldn't go over well.

"We don't have a lot of choice. Santa One is still in isolation with the flu. And Reverend Wong has commitments tomorrow, but he can make the dinner and dance."

"So, Rory it is," Lauren said. "He'll make a terrific Santa, if he isn't grumpy. He sure looks the part."

David grunted. "I thought so, too. Which is why, when Santa One got sick, Rory was going to be Santa. Then, he stepped in that Baxter trap outside Community Hall."

"But he's just gotten out of the hospital. Did you talk to Dr. Fleming about it?"

David nodded. "I did. Rory was mostly in the hospital so they could care for him until he got his walking boot. Dr. Fleming wanted him off his feet."

Lauren took all that in. "How did you ever convince Rory Hardin to be Santa?"

"You look positively shocked."

"Truthfully, I am." She dipped her chin. "Rory doesn't like social gatherings."

"True," David said. "Which is why I recruited Caroline to ask him. He'll do anything for Caroline."

"You are sly, David Decker."

"I thought it was a stroke of genius. It gets us a Santa and it gets Rory and Caroline to the festivities."

"Brilliant." Lauren smiled up at him.

He smiled back, and for a second, longing flooded his eyes, and he leaned toward her.

Inside, she was shaking. "Barbara?" Lauren called out. Had he been about to kiss her? No, he couldn't have been. Could he? "We're in a hurry." Maybe that lean in had been due to his leg. Or just a trick of the light. Relieved and disappointed, and grateful she'd been spared another regret, she called again. "Barbara?"

"Sorry." Barbara rushed in with Baxter at her heels. "I just had to check and make sure he hadn't picked up any thorns. They can be very painful, you know."

"I'm sure they can be," David said. "Baxter okay?"

"Oh, he's fine. Just fine." She seemed a little flustered. "Now where did I put the paperwork." She ruffled through a short pile. "Hmm, not there."

"Just write some notes," Lauren suggested. When Barbara grabbed a pen and pad, Lauren reeled off the items on her mother's list. First for the parade, then the sleigh rides, the roses for the bonfire, and then the largest of the orders for the dance. When she disclosed placement, right from the planning sheet, Barbara looked stunned.

"Well, that's…perfect," Barbara said, her jaw slightly agape.

"What's wrong?" Lauren asked, certain now that her mother and Barbara Pope had already discussed exactly what she'd wanted.

"Not a thing." Barbara gave her a stilted smile. "This will work beautifully."

"Not short on poinsettias?" Lauren asked, glancing at Baxter, who was sporting a bright red bowtie with a bell around his neck. "After losing a few to stomping?"

"No. No, we'll be fine."

"Lucky for you, Baxter." David dipped down to scratch his ruff.

"With Baxter in the shop, you know to prepare for little incidents." Barbara shrugged. "One of the joys of being his pet human."

David laughed. "I guess we're done here, then?"

"Yes. Yes, you are." Barbara's face turned bright red. "We'll handle the rest."

Lauren nodded, turned to David. "We'd better get the tickets to the business owners, then."

"Right." He smiled at Barbara. "Tomorrow is the big day, and there's still so much to do."

Barbara sent a knowing look at Lauren, then turned her gaze back to David. "Isn't that always the way of things? Nine million little details."

Lauren and David left the shop and, out on the sidewalk, David paused. "We need to get the tickets from my car."

"I'll do that. You rest your leg."

"It's okay."

"It is, but we have a lot of walking to do, and the snow isn't helping." Heavy flurries fell and stuck. "No sense taking risks we don't need to take. You'll get a workout in delivering the tickets."

"True." He accepted with dignity. "I'll wait here."

"Granny's would be better," she said. "Out of the cold, and I need another coffee. This job requires caffeine."

"You never drink caffeine." He said it before thinking.

He remembered how she liked her coffee. Did that mean anything? "I allow myself one caffeinated cup every morning. The rest is decaf."

"Ah, changes."

"Unavoidable," she said. "Meet you there." She took his keys and headed off to get the tickets.

By noon, they had delivered the tickets around Town Circle and dropped by Granny's to grab a little lunch. When David slid into the booth near the front window, he winced.

"You okay?" Lauren asked, opening her napkin and folding it over her lap.

"You were right. That was quite a workout in fresh snow." He glanced out the window, where the snowfall was heavier now.

"I'm sorry," she said. "Is it really bad?"

"No, just uncomfortable. I do fine on certain surfaces, but ice and snow can be slick, and slick is rough."

"How did you pull the muscle? Mountain biking?" He used to be a huge fan of that.

"No." He avoided her gaze. "It was an accident."

"What kind of accident?"

He wanted to answer, but something seemed to hold him back. She waited, and finally he decided what he wanted to say.

"An ill-timed one. Stupid, really. I was in a place I shouldn't have been at a time I should have been elsewhere. Had I known then what I know now, trust me, it would have been avoided."

Cryptic. That he regretted the incident was clear. Stuck with a cane and a limp, who wouldn't regret it? "I expect most accidents are regarded that way. Best if avoided."

"I suppose so. Though, some are more costly than others." He lifted the menu. "What's for lunch?" His voice brightened. "I'm starved."

So was she. Her stomach had been growling for half an hour. "Granny's vegetable soup for me." Lauren couldn't resist. "It's absolutely the best, and maybe by the time I get it down, I'll thaw out."

"It's pretty cold out."

"Freezing." She stuck out her hand.

He grasped it, gently squeezed her fingers. "Frozen."

She smiled and withdrew her hand.

Bailey Adams, the current owner of Granny's appeared at their table. "David, I've mapped out the route for the sleigh ride. You want to come by later this afternoon and check it out."

"Sure." He glanced at Lauren. "We have to be at the caterer at six o'clock," he told Lauren. "Kenneth's got the dinner ready for us to sample."

"That's fine," she said. "Should I come with you to check the sleigh route?"

"I can handle that," David said. "I'm sure you'd like to visit your mom."

"I would, if you're sure."

"Absolutely." He looked back at Bailey. "What time is the lunch crush over?"

"About two o'clock, if that fits your schedule."

"I'll meet you there."

Bailey nodded, glanced at them both. "I don't know what you two are doing different, but ticket sales are through the roof on all the events."

"Really?" Lauren was pleased. "I haven't had time to check the site, but everyone is increasing their order."

"We're getting folks from two counties over," Bailey said. "The inn's totally booked, and the motel near the park is, too."

"That's a good sign." David smiled at Lauren.

"Whatever it is, keep it up," Bailey said. "We need the funds for the music program, but we sure could use a school nurse, too."

"That's a great idea," David said, turning again to Lauren. "Mrs. Wong wants to be an RN."

"She's been an LPN for years." So far as Lauren knew, there'd been nothing that had come up she hadn't been able to handle.

"The kids need an RN, she says." David shrugged. "She's done as much as she can do online, but she's got some practical experience to get before she earns her degree."

"Can she do it and be back to school in the fall?"

Bailey answered. "If she can take leave the last two weeks of school, she'll be done in time for the next school year. But she refuses to leave the kids unless someone steps in and takes over."

"Maybe we could hire a temp or something like that," David suggested.

"Can't find one. At least, we haven't yet. The school board has looked high and low, but no luck so far. What we need is a Christmas miracle. Maybe you two can figure something out. You're doing great on the festivities." Bailey turned and returned to the kitchen.

Lauren did have an idea.

"What?" David asked Lauren.

She snapped her gaze to him. "Excuse me?"

"You've got that look."

"What look?"

"The one that says you have an idea." She opened her mouth and he wrinkled his nose. "Don't deny it. I know you too well. What's the plan?"

"It probably won't work," she said. "It's asking a lot."

"What is?"

"Reverend and Mrs. Wong do so much to help others in the community. I can't believe others wouldn't step up for them."

"They likely would, if they knew there was a need and why. She's doing this RN thing for the Ridge kids, not for herself. I say we go for it." He leaned toward her over the table. "Who can refuse you when you get that look?"

He had refused her. But why bother pointing that out. Besides, this was for the kids and for the Wongs, not for her. No community rallied better than Holt Ridge. "You're exactly right, David." Lauren smiled. "Nothing ventured, nothing gained."

"If any place will step up, my money is on the Ridge."

"Mine, too." She pulled out her phone. "Jess, it's Lauren. David and I need a favor…"

David waited expectantly until Lauren hung up the phone. "She's working on it." Lauren smiled.

"You think she'll come through?"

"I have a good feeling," Lauren said. "Jess reminded me that Mrs. Wong sewed Minnie's arm back on in third grade. She'll take two days of vacation time to fill in at school."

"Two down, eight days to go. That's great." David grinned. "Minnie? Who is Minnie?"

"Jessica's doll. She wagged that thing everywhere until Middle School. I suspect she carried her in her backpack straight through High School, though she'd never admit it."

"Seriously?"

"I suspect, I said." Lauren dropped her voice to a whisper. "Jessica freaked out at taking tests. Minnie was her good luck charm. Jessica never took a test without her."

"Bless Mrs. Wong for fixing her up, or Jessica might not be an RN today." David laughed hard.

So did Lauren. That had every head in Granny's pivoting to see what they found so funny.

"They're still gawking at us."

Lauren took a sip of water. "It's different."

"How?" David turned to the window. "They still all watch our every move."

"Yes, they do. But look at their faces. That's what's different."

David scanned the dining area, then looked back at her. "They do look different."

"It's not curiosity or waiting for a war to happen now."

"It's more than that," he said. "They look happy that we're getting along."

"As, I am sure, are we. It's so much easier on us all, isn't it? To get along well, I mean."

His expression softened. "Discord between us…it just feels wrong."

"It makes anything we have to do together harder."

"At least that hasn't changed. We've always gotten along well." He stopped, then his expression soured. "Except when I went off the rails."

Breaking up with her by text. Off the rails was a decent description. But the pain had left his face, and she didn't want to bring it back. "Past is past," she said, brushing the comment aside for both their sake's. "Finish your soup. It's getting cold."

He finally picked up his spoon and got started, which Lauren took to mean the pain in his leg had subsided enough that he could eat now. Grateful for that, she went to work on eating her own.

11

December 21st
1:30 PM

"MOM, you're awake and sitting up." Lauren smiled and entered the hospital room. "I'm so glad." The difference in the way she looked was profound. "The medicine is working."

"I told you it was." She smoothed her hair with her hand. "Jessica did my hair this morning after my bath. I have to tell you, few things in my life have felt as good."

"She's a wonder." Lauren sat down on the edge of the bed at its foot. "I have some news for you, if you're up to hearing it."

"Of course." She leaned back against the chair.

"Ticket sales are brisk. We're going to have enough to fund the music program and a little more."

"What little more?"

"Two weeks of nursing so Mrs. Wong can do her work on her RN to finish it up before school starts."

Her mother gasped. "Oh, Lauren, that's wonderful news. But who will nurse the kids the last two weeks? That's been the problem. Finding someone qualified to hire."

"Jessica took care of it." Lauren lifted a hand. "When the nurses found out what Mrs. Wong was doing, they wanted to help, so they're all taking a day or two of vacation time to fill in at school so Mrs. Wong can be sure the kids are taken care of and she can do what she needs to do."

"A Christmas miracle," her mother said, clapping her hands. "That Jessica is just a wonder."

"She is something else. Always has been."

"Does Mrs. Wong know yet?"

"David and I are going to tell her tonight, before we go to dinner."

Her mother sobered. "You have a dinner date with David?"

"No. No, it isn't a date. Kenneth Pope has the sample meal prepared for the Christmas dinner and dance. We have to sign off on it tonight, before he goes further with it."

"Why?" She seemed surprised. "We've never required a sample meal. Most of us have eaten Kenneth Pope's food all our lives."

"So, you didn't do that?" Lauren was more stunned than her mother.

"Of course not." Her expression backed up her words, and it was clear she was pretty peeved someone else had required it.

"And what about requiring two signatures to approve anything?"

"Like what?"

"The ticket design, the photographer, the flowers…"

Her eyes widened with every disclosure, but she quickly shielded them. "I, um, think that's wise, considering neither you nor David have planned these events on your own before."

She didn't have a clue about any of it. "Mom…?"

No answer.

Her eyes shut.

And she was asleep, or feigning sleep. She wasn't going to disclose a thing.

"Never mind. It's not important."

Her eyes opened.

Caroline had been right. Vanessa Holt was thinking, but she wouldn't share those thoughts. Lauren had recognized that look of her mother's her entire life. Little could wrestle a peep out of her. But maybe there was another path. "You know, last night when I went into your She Shack for the candy canes and ribbon, I found some papers…"

No change in her expression. Nothing clouding her eyes. "What kind of papers, dear?"

"Ones I would have expected to be in the planning packet but weren't."

"In my She Shack?" Confused, her mother shrugged. "I can't imagine."

"Mom, do you promise me you didn't take them out of the packet and put them on your work table?"

"Why in the world would I do that?"

"I have no idea." She kept her voice calm, unemotional. "Maybe to make David and I spend more time together?"

"No, Lauren." She rubbed at the edge of her robe between two buttons. "I think it's good that you and David are doing the festivities together, but I didn't put any papers from the packet into my She Shack. That is a fact."

Not a hint of motherly matchmaking.

Caroline. She was the only other person who had access to both Dad's home office, and Mom's She Shack. Time to drop the subject. "The good news is everyone has more ticket requests than they initially ordered, and the hotels are booked." And the locals weren't staring at David and her, expecting fireworks anymore. That was above and beyond just good news. It was another miracle. At least, it was in Lauren's book.

"And David?" Worry flashed across her mother's face. "Is he holding up okay?"

"He seems fine," Lauren said, taken aback by the odd question. "The snow and ice are making his limp more pronounced. He was in pain at lunch, but after he sat down for a while, it was better enough that he could eat."

"Did he tell you that?"

"It was impossible not to notice it."

"He promised me he wouldn't overdo, but I was afraid he would. It's the Christmas thing, I expect." She tasked, clicking her tongue to the roof of her mouth. "Lauren, you must make him slow down and get off his feet more."

"I can't do that." The idea mortified her. "I have no right to say anything about what he does or doesn't do. It's none of my business." What was the Christmas thing?

"Having compassion for a fellow human being you nearly married makes it your business. It's the right thing to do." Her eyes narrowed. "You have no idea how he suffers with that leg."

She was getting upset. And so was Lauren. "You're right, Mom. I don't have any idea. I don't even know how he was injured other than it was an ill-timed accident."

"Indeed it was, and isn't that enough?"

"Maybe it should be, but, no, it isn't." Too agitated to sit, Lauren stood and paced a short path between the foot of the hospital bed and the window. "The human being in me doesn't want to pry. But the bride dumped the night before her wedding demands details."

"I know you don't wish him harm. Goodness, Lauren, after all he's been through, that would be heartless."

"What has he been through…exactly?" Lauren asked.

Her mother stuttered, clearly flustered.

Afraid she'd pushed too far, Lauren backed off. "Never mind. Don't say a word. I'll ask him myself."

Relief washed over her mother's face. "Darling, I think that's a grand idea. Long overdue, and a grand idea."

12

December 21st
5:30 PM

THE PHONE RANG.

In her mother's kitchen, Lauren answered, "Hello."

"Lauren, it's David. How was your mom?"

After filling a tea cup, Lauren sat down at the breakfast bar. "She looks a lot better. Jessica was waiting on lab results to confirm it, but physical signs are the infection has stopped spreading and just maybe the antibiotics are kicking in."

"That's great. Does she look better?"

"Yes, she does."

"It's rattled me to see her like this. I can only imagine what it's done to you."

He really cared about her mother. Lauren could hear it in his voice. "I've had root canals that didn't make me as nervous."

"Did Jessica have any luck, finding nurses to help Mrs. Wong?"

"I texted you on that."

"Didn't get it."

Probably the weather. "It's done. People were signing up so fast, Jessica had to forfeit one of her two days. Everyone had a story of something wonderful Mrs. Wong had done for them or their kids and wanted to help."

"And that right there is one reason I love it here."

"Me, too." Was Holt Ridge big enough for both of them?

"She's going to be so excited."

She was. "I thought maybe we could stop by and tell her on our way to dinner."

"What if we announced it at the dance?" David said. "She's going to want to thank everyone."

"That'll work." Lauren nodded. "It'll be a nice touch, and it's good for the kids to see how the community comes together to help each other."

"Speaking of help," he said. "I, um, wondered if you'd do me a favor."

Now that was unexpected. "If I can."

"My leg has exceeded its daily dose. Would it be too much trouble for you to pick me up and we ride together to Pope's Catering? I know we agreed to meet there, but it would be best if I didn't drive anymore today."

"Of course. I'll be there in about fifteen minutes."

"Thank you, Lauren."

"No problem at all." She hung up the phone, certain his leg had to be killing him or he'd never ask for a favor, especially from her.

Caroline walked in and shrugged out of her coat, then went straight for the teapot. "It's wickedly cold out there."

"They're calling for more snow. One to two inches."

Lauren smoothed a hand over her black skirt and sweater top.

"I've been to see Rory. He's going to do the Santa stint, but I'm not sure the kids are ready for it. He's ticked to the nines."

"Why?"

"That's the thing. When I told him Reverend Wong would fill in if he couldn't handle it, he got really upset. He said he'd do it, and he intended to see it done."

"He's actually looking forward to it." Lauren gasped. The recluse forced to interact. "What else could explain that kind of reaction?"

"I don't get it," Caroline said.

"You don't have to," Lauren told her. "Just be there to keep him from snapping at the kids. He's supposed to be Santa. Someone who wants to see and spend time with them. No one can remind him like you."

"I wasn't planning on going."

"What you were planning isn't significant. I wasn't planning on being here and doing all I'm doing either."

Caroline frowned, but she knew she'd lost. "Fine."

"Fine." Lauren shrugged into her coat. "Oh, I have a question."

Caroline poured her tea. "Shoot."

"Did you take some papers out of Mom's planning packet and put them on the work table in her She Shack?"

"No." Standing at the stove, she turned toward Lauren. "You know I hate to go into that place. All that clutter gives me the creeps."

"Dad forbade it. That's why it creeps you out, but you went in last night."

"Just to grab the candy canes and get out of there."

That was true. "So, you didn't put the papers on Mom's work table?"

"No." Caroline lifted her cup. "What kind of papers were they?"

"Not important." Lauren said, wrapping her scarf at her neck. "Has anyone else been in there?"

"No, not that I know—wait. David," she said. "He put the candy canes and ribbons in there for Mom."

Shock rippled through Lauren's body. "So, if her mother hadn't done it, and Caroline hadn't done it… Lauren chided herself. David?

She was being ridiculous. Why on earth would David remove the papers and redo work he knew had already been done. That would be absurd. There had to be another explanation. He hadn't been any more eager than she about them working together on this. At least, at first. "Did anyone help him?"

"I'm not sure," Caroline said. "Paul Miller was out in the backyard with him, but whether or not he went into Mom's She Shack, I have no idea." She stretched her back. "If you're going to be at Pope's Catering at six, you better get a move on."

13

December 21st
5:45 PM

WHEN DAVID WAS SEATED in her mother's silver Navigator, Lauren closed the door. "Sorry. I got tied up last minute."

"We're good. We'll make it to Kenneth's by six." He shivered. "Man, the temperature is dropping like a rock."

"The weather report is warning of another two-inches of snow before morning." She pulled away from the curb in front of his house and tried to ignore the lump in her throat. It once was to have been their home. How Lauren had loved that house. She couldn't believe he'd bought it anyway. "Is that going to create any problems for the sleigh rides?"

"Bailey says, no. We looked at the route and I didn't see any danger areas, though I defer to him. Who better knows Hillside Park than Bailey Austin?"

"No one that I know of," Lauren agreed. "I love that park."

"It's special." David propped his cane between his knees, parked a hand on its handle. He'd been using it for a long while to position it so absently. "We couldn't ask for a better place for sleigh rides or the bonfire. The guys have been gathering wood for days."

"The fire chief has checked it all out, right?"

"This afternoon. Bailey had him come out while the two of us were there. We're set."

"And the vendors?"

"Start arriving early in the morning. It'll all be ready to go long before the Critter Parade."

She smiled. "I'll bet every kid on the Ridge is too excited to sleep."

David grunted. "I'll bet a lot of adults are, too. I am."

"Really?" She spared him a sidelong glance and braked to a stop at the corner Stop sign.

"Absolutely." He nodded. "I never had any of these traditions growing up. In our neighborhood, people didn't know their neighbors' names, much less interact."

"One of the pitfalls of big city living. It's like that in Atlanta, too. People pretty much stay to themselves."

"Another perk of living in Holt Ridge." He glanced out the side window.

"Is that why you came here and started your company?"

"It's one of many reasons," he said. "With my leg, I no longer work in the field, but I have staff all over the planet. They do the field work. That freed me up to choose where to live. My physical location doesn't impact the business at all."

"That's good."

"It is."

Curiosity burned and in it she summoned courage. "David, I take it from what you said your injury isn't a pulled muscle. It's permanent."

"It is."

"What happened to your leg?" He didn't respond, and she added, "I know you said it was an ill-timed accident. That you were somewhere you shouldn't have been, but what exactly does that mean?"

"I was injured on a job."

"Negotiating a contract?" That had been his specialty.

"Reviewing a site." He paused, then finally continued. "There was an equipment accident. I learned the hard way that a man is no match for a ton of machine."

She got chills all over. "You're lucky you lived."

He looked right at her. "I am."

Had the possibility he wouldn't live existed? Looking at his sober expression, she thought it might have. She pulled into Pope's Catering's parking lot. She had more questions, but the time for them had ended.

Maybe that was just as well. Her emotions were in turmoil. A world without David? She couldn't wrap her mind around it.

He was being deliberately evasive, too, which she'd never known him to be. But an accident that could have cost him his life and had left him permanently injured likely was too painful a memory to recall and discuss. He'd relive it every time. She couldn't do it. She shouldn't expect him to do it, especially when explaining wasn't necessary and she had no right to ask.

They went inside. Kenneth was seated at his desk in the little office in the back of the kitchen. "Come on back," he shouted out and then stood up. "Glad you got here okay. Snow's really coming down."

"The roads aren't bad," Lauren said, "but there sure is

a chill in the wind."

"Hope that passes before the Critter Parade. Baxter doesn't much like the cold. It'll make him a cranky host." Kenneth smiled but there was no humor in it.

Lauren glanced at David, then back at Kenneth. "I'm sure Barbara has a coat for him." Baxter had more clothes than most people.

"True." Kenneth rubbed his hands together. "You two ready to taste test the dinner for the dance?"

"Sure am." David said.

"I've set you up a table over there." He motioned to a quiet corner. "Go on and sit down."

The table was draped in white linen with a small floral arrangement as a centerpiece and a candle already lighted in its middle. "How pretty," Lauren said.

"Glad you like it." Kenneth turned to her. "All the tables will be set this way, of course. Barbara's handling that. Sit down. Sit down. Everything's ready."

As they worked their way through the meal, Kenneth stayed out of sight, which seemed a little odd. Lauren had several questions, like why there were three meat choices and a Vegan option. That seemed like a lot of extra work for an event.

"I'm making a list of questions we can ask. I think he's in his office on the phone."

"Ah," she said to David. "That explains that."

"So, tell me about your life in Atlanta." David tested a bit of roast beef. From his expression, he approved.

"I still teach. Third grade now instead of first. And I still love it. Aside from that, I work in a neighborhood garden in my spare time. James and I do. It's safer work as a team."

"Is James a neighbor or someone special in your life?"

"We've dated for a while. He's a good man, but I

wouldn't say he was special."

"What would you say?"

"He likes to garden." She hiked a shoulder. "And he has the potential to be special." That was true. He really was a great guy. Just not for her. She'd tried. She'd wanted to feel what she did with David, but she just didn't. Of course, there's no way she would reveal that to David.

"Will he be coming here for Christmas?"

She hadn't invited him. They weren't serious. They just did things together sometimes to avoid doing them alone. "His family gathers in Vermont every Christmas. He'll be going there."

"I see," David said, and she feared he really did. "I promised Reverend Wong I'd chaperone a youth group at the bonfire. I could use another set of eyes, if you're available."

Her lips curved in a sly smile. It faded to uncertainty.

"What?"

It was hard being with a man so attuned to your nuances. "Us being together at this outing could ramp up speculation about us. Do we want to risk it? They're just calming down."

"The different faces at Granny's."

Lauren nodded.

He tilted his head. "It could ramp up speculation, or it could put it to rest, which would be a good thing." David took a sip of wine. "I'll risk it if you will."

"Why not? I'd planned to be there anyway. Might as well make myself useful."

They finished their meal, lavished praise on Kenneth, and signed off, giving their approval. As they were leaving, Lauren asked, "Mr. Pope, who required this sample dinner?"

He stammered then lifted his arms. "You two are new

to this. Always a good idea. Keeps you from worrying."

No one had required it. He'd taken it on himself. "Well, it was wonderful. They're in for a treat."

"Thank you." He opened the door, signaling them to depart. She supposed he'd had a long day and was eager to wrap up and get home.

Back in the car, David snapped his seatbelt into place. "I ate way too much."

"So did I. But it was great." Quiet. Intimate. And she and David had fallen right into their old pattern of talking about anything and everything. And they'd laughed. Oh, but it'd been a long time since she'd laughed like that. She had the feeling that it had been a while for him, too.

Back at his house, she pulled to the curb and stopped. "We're all set for tomorrow?"

"Completely," he said. "I've run the checklists multiple times. We're ready."

"What time should I be at the park for the vendors?" she asked.

"I've got it covered. You'll need to help Tom and Sylvia get the critters in order for the parade. It's going to start on West Main, about two blocks down, go through the Circle, then on to Hillside Park. Awards will be given out from the stage there."

"Sounds great. So, noon is good?"

"Parade starts at two o'clock sharp, so noon should be fine. Others will handle things. You're just there to look reassuring, in case anything odd comes up." He grasped the handle of his cane. "I enjoyed our dinner, Lauren," he said softly. "To be honest, I was a little nervous about it."

She had been, too. "Why?" Throughout all of this, they'd gotten along well. And it wasn't the first meal they'd shared since her return.

He let her see pain in his eyes. "For all the reasons

you'd think."

When she started to respond, honestly having no idea what to say, he held up a forefinger. "Let me just say, thank you. You're an amazing woman and, under the circumstances, you couldn't be more gracious."

How did she respond to that? Thank you seemed trite. Anything else, ungracious. And she wasn't at all sure she wanted to be gracious. She wanted to flat-out demand he tell her why he'd sent that text and ended them. That's what she wanted to do…but she couldn't. It'd create all kinds of tension and they had a busy couple of days to get through.

Maybe by the end of them, she'd understand why he appealed her to in every way as much as he always had. As if he'd never shattered her heart and walked away. How did he do that?

How could she let him?

Love.

Feeling very much at its mercy, she nodded. "It's been different than I expected," she told him. "I'm glad about that."

"So am I." He stepped out of the car, closed the door and limped to his front door, then disappeared inside.

"Lauren Holt, you're an idiot. Why didn't you just ask him? He was waiting for it. Expecting it."

She pulled out into the street and headed home. "Maybe, just maybe, you're not ready to hear his answers."

Sad truth was, maybe she wasn't. After everything that had happened here after the breakup, the last thing she needed was to learn it had been her fault. Guilt flooded her. It might have been. She'd gotten so wrapped up in the wedding, she'd lost track of the man. She hadn't seen that then, but she saw it clearly now. And maybe that's why he'd texted them getting married would be a mistake.

14

December 22nd
12:00 PM

Tom and Sylvia's son, Paul Miller, assisted Binks in getting the lineup settled in two blocks from center circle, in front of the library. Binks would get great candid shots of the Critters Christmas Parade as the contestants entered the circle.

There were, of course, a few little hitches, but nothing major that wasn't resolved in just a few minutes. One of the Adams boys lost the wheel on his wagon, and his bloodhound, Thirsty, wasn't much enjoying the bumpy ride, but Tom Miller ran over to his hardware store and had Thirsty's ride rolling smooth in no time.

The costumes put smiles on everyone's faces. Baxter led the procession into the circle. He was dressed as Santa with the exception of him sporting a red bow tie and a dapper cap instead of the typical Santa hat. Barbara confided Kenneth hadn't wanted to confuse the kids into thinking Baxter was really Santa.

Someone's cat, Lauren had no idea whose, rode with Baxter in a bicycle cart. It was female and dressed as Mrs. Claus.

"This is really something," David said from beside her.

"I think it's my favorite event of all." Lauren laughed. "Everything okay at the park?"

"Ready and waiting," he said.

Lauren scanned the critters coming into the circle. "I thought you only issued a few waivers."

"I did."

She cast him a doubtful look. "I'm seeing a lot more than cats and dogs, David. I'm seeing a turtle—"

"I told you about the turtle."

He had. "And a goat, and is that Rory's mule?"

David stammered. "Rory's playing Santa at the events and he just got out of the hospital with the bad ankle. He's not too happy, having to wear the boot and use crutches. I couldn't very well tell the man Hark wasn't welcome."

"Hark?" Lauren asked.

"Rory's mule," David said. "Hark."

"Uh-huh. Keeping Baxter out of dog jail, is more like it."

"True, but that's an added perk." He gave her an angelic smile.

"And two raccoons, a squirrel, a parrot and—oh my word." She gasped and grabbed his sleeve. "David, tell me you didn't let anyone enter a snake."

"Calm down. It's fake." David looped their arms and leaned close then whispered, "I told Bailey Adams to toss it in so maybe you wouldn't be too upset about the other interlopers."

"David Decker, you deliberately deceived me?"

"Never," he said. "Distracted you, yes. I did. But I did not deceive you."

A stir at center circle claimed Lauren's attention. "Oh-oh. Baxter's abandoning his post." He hopped down from the bicycle cart and made a beeline for the 42' White Pine tree half the town spent time decorating. Growling, he chomped down on the shiny red garland, and then he started tugging.

"Kenneth!" Barbara ran toward the tree. "Baxter, stop that. If you pull the tree over, you're going to hurt someone." She scanned the circle. "Kenneth! Baxter's going to cut his mouth on that garland. Do something."

The parade halted while Kenneth chased down Baxter and returned him in all his splendor to the cart. Bits of garland clung to his Santa beard. This time, Kenneth left Baxter's leash on and clipped it to the cart. He wouldn't be able to jump out again.

Barbara rushed over to them. The parade waited and no one moved until Barbara checked Baxter's mouth and made sure there were no cuts.

"No one is complaining," David said. "Don't you find that odd?"

"Not at all." Lauren watched Barbara back away from the bicycle cart and announce that Baxter was fine. Such relief crossed her face. "He's a pain," Lauren said, "but he makes the Popes happy. That matters most, so everyone indulges them."

"Janelle." David said, remembering that the Popes had lost their only child.

Lauren nodded. "Baxter can do anything and it's just fine. No one wants to see either of them ever again as torn up as they were then. It was heartbreaking."

"Baxter may be fine, but the garland is history. He's chewed it to bits."

"The tree is still standing. That's a win." Lauren smiled up at David.

"Why are there so many white ornaments with gold glitter?" he asked. "Crosses, snowflakes, doves, butterflies, stars—is that a shepherd's crook?"

"It is," Lauren said. "There are fish, shells and chalices, too."

"There's a story behind them, isn't there?"

"There's a story behind each one of them," she said. "My mother saw them in Virginia, and when she married my dad, she started a tradition here. They're Chrismons—the white and gold ornaments. Those are the liturgical colors of the Christmas season."

"I'm seeing Mrs. Wong's touch in these, too."

"Actually, you are. Every year, Mom and Mrs. Wong make a Chrismon for each child. They're cut from white Styrofoam. It's an annual youth group project. The kids choose the design they want and then they decorate it with gold glitter. Each of the designs is an ancient symbol for Christ or his ministry."

"An apt tradition for Christmas."

"After all these years, it's such an ingrained tradition in the community, it wouldn't seem like Christmas without it." Lauren smiled. "One of those Chrismons is mine."

"They keep them all?" David seemed surprised.

"They do, and every year, when the tree is being decorated, there's a lot of people searching to find their Chrismon. Kids and adults."

"I like that tradition. It creates a real sense of belonging, and of a personal history in the community." David stared a long moment at the tree. "Maybe one day I'll have a Chrismon hanging there, too."

"I'd be shocked if you don't already." His jaw dropped,

and Lauren smiled. "My mother probably put one on the tree for you the first year you were here."

"You think so?"

"You'll have to ask her to be sure, but let's just say, it would be very unlike her not to have done one for you."

"Let's go look for them."

He seemed so excited; Lauren couldn't refuse.

She spotted hers in the first few minutes. "My angel."

"How do you know it's yours?"

"My name's on the back. I guess I forgot to share that part. When you finish decorating, you write your name on the back with the marker. Some use a paint pen." She smiled up at him. "So you can always tell your Chrismon is yours."

"I really like this tradition."

It took a solid half-hour to locate David's. But there it was, his name written in marker on its back, just like everyone else's. "I found it," he said excitedly. "Lauren, look. I found it."

She moved closer, but his hand shielded the ornament. "What is it?"

"I'm an angel, too." He sounded a little breathless, a little awed.

"Told you she'd have done one."

"Funny," he said. "I never expected an angel."

"I was told she thinks of you as her son."

David looked over at Lauren and blinked hard. "I almost was."

"Almost." Lauren repeated, but there was no heat in her tone. Only regret. And from the sound of David, in that moment, at least, he regretted, too.

"Your mother is really something," he said. "That angel… including me. It's one of the nicest things anyone has ever done for me."

Emotional. Very emotional. "You're a good man. I'm sure there have been many nice things in your life."

"Not like this. Never like this."

The reason he was so moved came to her. "I'd forgotten your family didn't celebrate Christmas."

"It was too much work, and we were too much trouble. I guess that's why I get so involved in the festivities now. All those Christmases of nothing. I need to catch up."

"I hope you never catch up, David." Lauren caught herself and grimaced. "Sorry. I didn't mean that the way it sounded." Her chilled face burned hot. "It's just that you're so full of wonder and awe at Christmas. I hope you never lose that. It's a beautiful thing, and it's contagious."

"Christmas is a time when anything can happen. Anything at all."

Nothing is impossible at Christmas. Familiar words. Her mother's words. "Maybe it is." Lauren smiled.

"I guess we should get over to the park. The front of the parade will be arriving there soon, and the voting will start for the best costume."

"Okay." She fell into step beside him and they made their way through the crowd of people around the circle to City Hall, then took the wide walkway to Hillside Park.

"The weather is gorgeous today, isn't it?"

"It is. I didn't dream it'd be this nice, considering last night. For a while, the snow was blowing horizontally." She noted his limp was getting more pronounced. "All this walking… is it too much for the leg?"

"It's getting a little stiff." Walking into the wind, he dipped his chin. "Walking usually isn't that bad, but combined with the cold, it gets rough. It's fine, though. I don't want to miss a second of this."

The boy in the man, reveling in Christmas pleasures. "Lean on me." She offered him her arm.

He took it.

The open expanse leading into the park proper was filled with snowmen, miniature reindeer and a red sleigh. Blue, gold, red and green ornaments that had to each be five feet in diameter littered the snow-covered lawn between the trees. Silver icicles hung from low-slung branches like moss. "This is adorable," Lauren said. "Who did it?"

"The high school kids. They did everything from where you leave the circle all the way to the park gate."

"Outstanding job." Lauren made a mental note to be sure to mention it to her mother, so some earned praise got back to the kids. They'd put their hearts into this project. Lauren pulled out her phone and snapped a few photos as a reminder and a memory. She took one of David, standing next to a snowman nearly as tall as he was, its carrot nose, the same shade of orange as his neck scarf. He looked…gorgeous, but something more. Happy. Really happy.

A few minutes later, they entered the gate to the park. Huge pine wreaths with cones and large red ribbons hung on each side. Beyond it, to the left was a life-size Nativity scene, and to the right, Bailey Adams sat in his sleigh waiting for riders to arrive. "Ready and waiting," he shouted to them. "You and Lauren ready for a ride?"

"Later," David said. "We have to check on the voting."

"Baxter will win," Lauren said so only David could hear. "He always wins."

"I know the mutt is in every Ridger's heart, but he hosted the parade. He can't win this year."

Lauren fretted. "Barbara will be disappointed."

"Actually," David covered her hand on their looped arms. "She removed him from the competition."

"Really?" Lauren didn't bother trying to hide her shock.

David grinned. "It would be unseemly for the host to win again."

"That's a Kenneth remark."

"It was." David waved to Paul Miller, driving the cart with Baxter and Mrs. Claus. The parade was hitting the park. "But Barbara agreed, after she got over the shock." He chuckled.

Bailey's sleigh horse whinnied, and Bailey shouted. "Come on, kids. Load up and let's go."

"I missed Rory at the parade. He is here, right?" Lauren scanned the grounds and spotted the wood stacked for the bonfire. The short safety fence surrounding it looked sturdy enough to keep the little ones away. The Fire Marshall would be satisfied, especially with a firetruck parked strategically close by.

"There." David pointed to the gap between the bonfire and the vendors selling balloons, funnel cakes, hot cider and cocoa and hotdogs.

"Ah, good." She walked on at David's side. "Rory might be a recluse, but being Santa was really important to him, so I'm glad his ankle is letting him do it."

"He's not moving around much, but I don't think an Act of Congress or the Council could have stopped him from playing Santa."

"Odd, isn't it?" she said. "The rest of the year, he can't abide being around other people, but at Christmas..."

David bent to whisper close to her ear. "Anything is possible. Even the grumpiest citizen in Holt Ridge playing Santa."

Binks had her camera set up on a tripod ready to photograph the kids on Santa's lap. She had streaked her hair red and green in honor of the occasion and waved at them. Lauren waved back.

"David." Barbara Pope came rushing over to them, a little breathless. "Can you help? Baxter's had a little… incident."

"What kind of incident?" Lauren asked.

"One that involves candy canes and ribbons and has Rory Hardin threatening to leash him to a tree until the bonfire's over." She shrugged. "Baxter loves peppermint. Why Rory didn't unwrap one for him, I have no idea. This whole incident could have been avoided."

"I'd better go see what I can do," David told Lauren.

She nodded. "I'm going to check with the craft vendors. I'm hoping Liz Baker's selling some of her apple butter."

"Is it good?" David asked. "I love apple butter."

"The best in three counties." She walked on toward the tent tops in the crafts section, passing a long line of teens waiting to get their faces painted.

15

December 22nd
5:00 PM

RORY'S NOSE stayed out of joint most of the afternoon with everyone except the kids. With them, he didn't express so much as a hint of grumpy behavior. Lauren wondered why he couldn't be that way more of the time.

Caroline explained it. "He doesn't want to need anyone. When you need someone and they leave you, it never stops hurting. So, it's better to just never start needing them."

"Is that what you do?" Lauren looked at her sister. Her nose and cheeks were bright red from the cold. She and their dad had been so close. Caroline grieved hard. It made sense that she would shut people out to avoid that kind of pain again, but oh, Lauren hoped she wasn't doing that.

"This isn't about me, it's about Rory."

"I know what we were talking about, but I want to know if that's why you avoid people, Caroline? Because if it is, you need to know there's more to that story. Yes, you might spare yourself from getting hurt. People could leave. But some might stay, and those who do can bring you a lot of joy. You're giving up all the good because there might be—might be—some bad. That's not fair, Caroline. Not to you or to the others who could benefit from all you could share with them."

She stuffed her gloved hands into her jacket pockets. "I hadn't looked at it that way, but I'll think about it."

"Good." That was a big concession from her sister, so Lauren didn't push.

"Speaking of hurt," Caroline said, looking beyond Lauren's shoulder, "here comes David."

Lauren turned and David joined them, smiling. "I bear good news."

"What's that?" Lauren smiled back.

"Hark won the best costume, and Rory is now in a really good mood."

"He was the cutest mule I've ever seen, dressed as an elf."

"Hark won?" Caroline gasped. "I made his costume. Oh, I have to go congratulate Hark—and Rory." She rushed off.

"I don't think I've ever seen her that animated." David watched her go.

"It's rare and usually involves Rory." Lauren chuckled. "I thought for a long time, if he were twenty years younger, he and Caroline would pair up."

"No, it's more a father thing."

"You think?"

She mentioned the mule first," David reminded Lauren.

Caroline had. "She always did like animals more than people."

"Did you see the hawk exhibition?"

"I missed that," she said. "Lys's hawk, right?" Lys was Tom and Sylvia Miller's granddaughter, and she had a way with hawks.

David nodded. "Bliss. That's the hawk she had with her today."

"Let me guess. You issued Bliss a waiver."

He cringed. "I did, but you would have, too."

A hawk is neither a dog nor a cat, David."

"But Lys saved her allowance for weeks and took Bliss down to Kay's Salon and got her a manicure. Her talons were white with green trees and red dots for ornaments. Could you refuse her?"

"Not a dog or a cat," Lauren repeated.

"But, Lauren, it's Christmas."

She smiled over at him. "You're right. I couldn't have refused her. Lys would have gotten her waiver."

"Bliss came in second."

"Second?" They stopped at the signpost for the sleigh ride. "Wow. I guess those talons were something else."

"They were. And Kay did a snowflake on Bliss's beak. Who would have thought a hawk would tolerate that without clawing?" David chuckled. "I asked how it went over with the other clients in Kay's salon—having Bliss there. Lys seemed baffled by the question."

"I'm betting no one batted an eye. And that Kay had nearly as many four-legged clients booked this morning as two-legged ones."

"I'm not touching that bet."

Lauren laughed. "Anything's possible at Christmas."

"It is in Holt Ridge." David glanced over at the mayor.

"They're about to light the bonfire." He offered his arm. "Walk with me?"

"Of course." Lauren looped their arms and they walked over. On the way, she noticed a lot of smiles turned in their direction. What that was all about, she had no idea. But between smiles and stares, she'd take smiles every time.

You're going to get hurt again. This closeness between you…it comes too easily.

She probably would. But she was already hurt, and this might be all she'd ever have with him. If that proved to be the case, she wanted as many memories to tuck into her heart as she could manage.

They'd have to last her a lifetime.

16

December 22nd
7:00 PM

THE MAYOR MADE a short speech about the traditions of the community and why they were important. He welcomed the guests, and then shared a little story of a Christmas long ago—the reason for the celebration. Even Reverend Wong was moved and dabbed at his eye with a paper napkin. The mayor reminded the kids they were on their honor not to get too close to the fire, and to stay well behind the fence, and then he lit the bonfire.

The blaze quickly caught, and flames licked at the wood, lit up the sky. The warmth from it washed over the crowd in welcome waves. "Doesn't the heat feel good?" Lauren asked David.

"It does." Standing close, he looped their arms.

The distant voices of carolers singing *Joy to the World* came closer and closer. The observers joined in. Standing semi-circle near Santa, the carolers went from song to song, singing old favorites.

"There you are, David." Tom Miller tugged at his cap. "The mayor's trying to call you."

"Everything all right?"

Tom shrugged. "Best I can tell, everything except your phone ain't working."

"Thanks." David pulled his phone from his pocket and then checked. "Battery's dead."

"You've been on it more than not all day," Lauren said, then passed him her phone. "Use mine." She hooked a thumb toward the vendors. "I've got to run over to the tents for a second. Be right back."

"If I'm not here, look for the mayor."

Lauren scooted between people, making her way out of the crowd. Liz Baker was holding a jar for her, and Lauren needed to get it before Liz sold it. Lauren had Caroline work out a deal for her and, while the terms settled on were steep, seeing that wonder and awe again would be worth it.

It'd make a great memory.

DAVID OPENED LAUREN'S PHONE AND SAW A MESSAGE from himself. Curious, he clicked on it, and saw the text he'd sent her the night before their wedding, breaking off, telling her he wouldn't be returning. His heart clenched in his chest. Why had she kept it all this time?

Knowing Lauren, she'd listened to it often, trying to make sense of his actions. That would be just like her.

He clicked over to voice mail and saw his own name again. Saw the voice mail he had left her days before sending the text. He listened to it, heard his joy at marrying her in a few days. The amazement he'd felt that of all the men in the world, she'd chosen to spend her life with him.

Guilt and regret bore down on him. He had broken her heart.

And his own.

He closed voice mail and paused, his emotions churning at what could have been, what almost was, what they both had wanted…then. Did she still want those things? A life with him?

She had kept the messages. Both of them. That had to mean something. But he doubted it meant that. How could she forgive him after what he'd done?

But she had kept both messages.

Why wouldn't she have deleted them long ago? She sure as certain hadn't needed a reminder of the heartache, or the risks of loving someone. He knew from experience, losing someone you love…you can't forget it no matter how hard you try. So why had she kept them?

He wanted to know. Not knowing why gnawed at him. Yet he had no right to ask. None. He'd forfeited asking anything from or of her with his handling of ending their relationship.

But keeping them had to mean something. He worried his lip, stared into the fire. Was it possible? Could there be a chance? A glimmer of hope?

Seeing her coming his way, he quickly dialed the mayor. They wrapped up their discussion just as she returned.

The look in her eyes. Soft. Caring. The way she used to look at him.

Maybe the glimmer was there. A spark of hope. If they had the courage to seek it. Did they?

Did he?

17

December 22nd
7:00 PM

SOMETHING WAS DIFFERENT. It was in his eyes.

David passed Lauren her phone. "Thanks."

The phone. The messages. Had he seen the messages?

Her heart beat hard and fast. She strongly suspected that's exactly what had inspired the change in him.

Minutes passed, but he didn't say anything about the messages, and there was no way she would bring them up. What would he think if he knew she'd revisited them every night, looking for answers in them she would never find?

He'd think she'd lost her mind. That's what he'd think. "Everything okay?"

David glanced over at her with a gentleness she'd never seen in anyone else's eyes on looking at her. A tenderness she hadn't seen in such a long time. "The mayor…?" She prodded him.

"Oh, the mayor. Everything's fine. He just wanted to tell us the safety fence was a great idea."

"Good." David wasn't smiling. Neither could she. Something had changed. It had to be the messages. What else could it be?

"Are you ready for that sleigh ride?" he asked.

She nodded. "If we skip it, Bailey Adams will serve us cold food at Granny's for weeks."

"Can't risk that, considering I eat more often there than at home."

"Why?" she asked, as he hooked their arms and they walked to the sleigh ride. "You're a great cook."

"It's not as much fun as it once was," he said.

"You don't like cooking anymore?" That surprised her.

"Oh, no. I still love to cook." He dropped his voice. "I just can't stand to eat alone."

"I totally get that." She sighed. "It gets old fast."

He grunted. "It's the lack of good conversation. I just wolf down the food and get out of the kitchen as fast as I can."

"At least you make it to the kitchen," she said. "I usually don't."

"But you are eating?" Worry crossed his face. "Not just junk food."

"I eat. I just don't enjoy it much anymore." They'd had some of their best conversations ever over meals.

"Remember our life, death and universe talks?" He looked away. "I loved those."

They had talked about everything and nothing—often at the same time. "Me, too."

"Whoa, Thirsty." Bailey Adams tugged at the reins and stopped near the signpost. "I was wondering if you two would make it over here." He pulled out a thermos and filled his cup. It smelled like hot chocolate.

"You staying warm?" David guided Lauren into the sleigh then stepped up and sat down beside her.

"Sure am. There's a blanket for your knees."

Lauren reached for it, then draped it across their laps. "Got it, Bailey. Thanks."

With a click of his tongue, Bailey jiggled the reins, and Thirsty started off on the course.

Soon, the singing voices faded, and the silence of the night surrounded them. Moonlight fell softly on the snow. Lauren sat close to David's side. "I'd forgotten how beautiful it is out here. And how quiet."

"The quiet is why I came to Holt Ridge."

"I wondered about that. You were always at home in the city."

"I was until the injury," he said, glancing off across a field. "After all the surgeries were behind me and the healing progressed beyond expectations, I needed a quiet place to reflect and recuperate. Holt Ridge seemed like the perfect place to heal."

"It is a slower pace, and a lot quieter," she said. "When exactly was that?"

He looked over at her. "About six months after you moved to Atlanta." He paused, then added. "You weren't living here anymore, so I didn't think being here would interfere in your life."

"You always did love coming to the Ridge."

"I did. I still love it here."

The door to this conversation was finally open, and she was definitely walking through it. "So, you moved here and started your own business."

"I did."

"And it's going well?" Over soup at Granny's, he'd said he had staff all over the planet.

"Exceeding expectations on all fronts. Easier to do when you hire great people."

"I can see where that would make all the difference."

"Lauren." His tone went serious. "Full disclosure." When she nodded, he continued. "I did know you weren't living here anymore, but I also knew, with your mother and Caroline still here, you'd return sometime."

"Yet you came here anyway."

"I did."

"Why, David?"

He hesitated a long time before answering. Anticipation built inside her. She knew the answer to this question would be significant. How? She had no idea, but it would matter.

He clasped her hand in his. "Because I knew when you returned, you'd be bringing home Christmas."

"I don't understand." She didn't dare read anything into his statement.

"At Christmas, we return to the things we hold closest in our hearts."

A simple but powerful message she totally understood. "Home," she said.

He nodded, leaning close, as if about to kiss her. Their gazes locked and Lauren caught herself leaning toward him. This might be a mistake. Another regret.

But it might not be. It might be glorious.

The sleigh stopped abruptly, jarring them.

Startled, Lauren looked over. They were stopped at the signpost. The ride was over.

David put the blanket on the opposite seat. "Thanks, Bailey."

"Sure thing." He looked back. "Well, did you two kiss?"

"What?" David asked.

Bailey lifted a hand. “I need to know. I’ve got a bet with Rory.”

Lauren snickered. “How much is the bet?”

Bailey blurted it out. “Five dollars and two jars of Liz Baker’s apple butter.”

She pecked a kiss to David’s surprised lips. “You win.”

“Well, all right!” Bailey laughed.

David looked into her smiling eyes. “If Liz Baker’s apple butter is the best, and Bailey and Rory have five dollars on the line, we can do better than a peck.” He kissed her, and he did it right.

18

December 22nd
9:00 PM

COLLECTIVE SIGHS from the group of twenty or so waiting in line for sleigh rides shattered the glow of their kiss and jerked Lauren back to reality fast. The kiss had been reminiscent of those they'd shared when he loved her, and that had her heart wrenching and her plastering a smile on her face. "That should get you the win, Bailey," she said. "Thanks for the ride."

The crowd laughed and so did Bailey. "Thanks!" he said with real enthusiasm.

David noted her emotional shift immediately and sobered.

They left the ride, and as soon as they were out of earshot, she stopped and turned to him. "David, what are you doing? Why did you kiss me like that?"

He frowned. "I did what you did. Made sure Bailey won the bet."

"That's not what you did."

He slumped against his cane. Didn't answer.

"Look, maybe you don't remember the difference in that kind of kiss, but I do. You owe me the truth, at least about that."

"You're right, okay?" He sighed and looked over at her, his face shadowed by the moonlight filtering through the trees. "I didn't mean to upset you."

"What did you mean?" she asked. "Everyone here knows you walked out on me. Everyone. I was your mistake, remember?" A hard knot formed in her chest. "We were just getting past the stares and gawking, and now they'll start all over again."

"Which is exactly why I did what I did."

"What?" She couldn't believe her ears. "You want them to gawk and stare and whisper behind our backs?"

He clasped her folded arms, let her see the truth in his eyes. "I wanted them to know that it was me. My fault. That you were blameless, and I still think you're wonderful." When her expression didn't soften, he gazed off, then went on. "I know they gave you a hard time after…you know."

"You called off our wedding the night before it was to take place and disappeared."

"Yes." He looked back at her.

"By a stupid text message."

"That couldn't be helped, but it's not the point."

"What is the point?"

"I know the people here thought it was your fault. We know it wasn't. I did what I did, and I wanted them to know it wasn't you."

It wasn't her. Three haunted years of wondering, and he reveals that gem as if it is a small thing. "I know you don't expect me to thank you."

"That's the last thing I expect from you, Lauren," he said. "I have no right to expect anything from you. I was just trying to put the blame for us on me. That's where it belongs." He looked her in the eye. "I promise."

That took the starch out of her spine, and the heat out of her voice. "Okay. I believe you, and I suppose I should be grateful that you wanted to do that for me, but I dealt with it all then and I'll deal with the fallout from this, too."

"I am sorry I upset you." He started walking. "We're chaperones. We need to get back to check on the kids."

He was right, and the subject was closed. At least, for now. They walked back to the bonfire and joined the youth group. They seemed to be having a great time.

Caroline appeared at Lauren's side and passed her a jar. "Liz Baker says she squared this with Bailey, and he agreed to give up one jar for two out of next season's apple crop. Don't drop it or anything. She's sold out and taking orders."

"Thanks, Caroline." Lauren took the jar. "I went to pick it up, and she told me you'd already gotten it."

"Thought I better before someone else wheedled it out of her. Liz is vulnerable to sob stories. I'm heading home," Caroline said. "I've had all the social stimulation I can take for one day."

"It was good of you to keep Rory in line," Lauren said, then uncertainty crept into her voice. "He did stay in line and was civil to the kids, right?"

"Wonderful with them," she reassured her sister. "But I expect he'll be talking about taking Hark home shortly."

"Thank you."

"You're welcome." Caroline almost smiled before turning and walking away.

She could be a great sister when she chose to be, and she had gone to a lot of trouble for Lauren. The jar in her hand felt heavy. Her heart wasn't as light as it had been when they'd struck the deal.

David's laughter claimed her attention and Lauren walked back over to him. When a lull in the conversation permitted, she passed him the jar. "Merry Christmas."

"Apple butter." He smiled. "Thank you, Lauren."

"You're welcome."

"Do I dare to hope Liz Baker made this?"

"You do, and she did."

"I tried to buy a jar, but she was sold out," he said. "I'm third on the waiting list for next year." He lifted an eyebrow. "How did you manage to get your hands on a jar?"

Her face burned. She'd rather not disclose that, especially after the spat they'd had over his kiss, but it seemed she'd have no choice. He stood waiting, expecting an answer. "You know that peck of a kiss I gave you?"

"Not likely to forget it."

"That was the fee for a jar."

He narrowed his eyes, but there was no anger in his voice. He was amused. "You are in so much trouble."

"I guess I am, but my intentions were good."

"So were mine, Lauren."

He wasn't talking about the kiss. He was talking about more. Maybe the more she'd wondered about for the last three years.

Someone tapped on her shoulder.

Lauren turned and saw Barbara Pope. "May I borrow you for a moment?"

"Of course." Lauren welcomed the interruption and

stepped away with Barbara. She'd had enough emotional turmoil for one day, especially with David. "Do you need something?"

"I'm information gathering to report to your mother. You know she's curious about everything going on here, and I don't want her feeling left out."

"That's very thoughtful of you."

Barbara flipped a hand. "Nothing she hasn't done for the shut-ins for years."

"I didn't know that." Her mother never ceased to amaze Lauren.

"I expect there's a lot you don't know, which brings me to why I interrupted you and David."

"No interruption."

She stiffened, but kept her thoughts on that to herself. "Has David told you yet what happened—before your wedding?"

"What do you mean?" Surely, she didn't mean what Lauren thought she did.

"Did he tell you why he called off the wedding?" Barbara asked, being even more blunt.

"You know why he called off the wedding?" Lauren answered with a question of her own. Barbara Pope meant exactly what Lauren thought she meant.

She studied Lauren's expression. "Um, never mind. I can tell by the look on your face, he hasn't told you yet." She clasped Lauren's upper arm. "Maybe you want to give him a little nudge on that, sweetie."

"A nudge?"

Barbara nodded. "Just to be honest, Kenneth and I have a little wager." She dipped her chin. "You know we've always seen you and David as a younger version of us and our relationship."

"You've mentioned it." About a thousand times. "If I may ask, what's the wager?"

"I think David still loves you. Kenneth says it doesn't matter. You'll never give him a second chance."

Lauren rolled her gaze. "Loves me?" She guffawed. "Barbara, David doesn't even know me anymore."

"Oh, sweetie, you're wrong about that," Barbara assured her. "David knows far more than you think…and if you don't know that, you know far less than you ought to know."

"I can't dispute that, but…"

She patted Lauren's arm. "Just give him a little nudge. Encourage him just a wee little bit."

Loves her? The woman had her feet in the clouds, engaging in a fanciful dream Lauren couldn't afford. She had to keep both feet firmly on the ground. "I can't do that."

She laughed. "Of course, you can."

From behind Barbara came all-too-familiar shouts. "Baxter!"

"What has that rascal gotten into now?" Wide-eyed, Barbara spun and took off toward the shouts at her mischievous mutt.

An hour later, the last of the kids was dropped off at his home and shortly thereafter Lauren pulled to the curb at David's. "There you go."

"Thanks," he said, lifting his cane. "And thanks again for this." He tucked the jar of apple butter into his coat pocket. "See you tomorrow at the dance."

"I'll be there." She smiled. "Good night."

He got out, shut the door and walked up the stairs to his entry door. He was dragging his leg, not limping. He'd definitely overdone it today.

He waved and went inside.

Lauren drove on home, their conversations replaying in her mind.

Their conversations, and their kisses.

19

December 23rd
8:00 AM

THE DOORBELL RANG.

Lauren was on her first cup of coffee, caffeinated, and still in her pajamas and robe. She peeked through the side-window and saw David, then opened the door. "You're out and about early this morning."

He limped in carrying a bouquet of yellow roses. "I just left your mother at the hospital."

"Coffee?"

He nodded, then sat down at the breakfast bar. "Finally, she's turned the corner, Lauren. The medicines are working." He smiled. "Jessica is encouraged. Actually, she's hopeful."

Touched by his relief, even though she didn't want to be, Lauren set a steaming mug of coffee before him. "It's the best news, she said. "Jessica called about half an hour ago to let me know the danger has passed."

"Whew." He shook his head. "I hope she doesn't scare me like that again for a long time."

He was genuinely fond of her mother. That was clear. Visiting her twice a day and his relief was stark. It couldn't be anything but sincere. "Why are you carrying flowers?"

He looked at them as if surprised to see them in his hand. "Oh, I got sidetracked. Yellow roses were always your favorites."

"They still are." Across the bar, standing in the kitchen, she leaned against the counter.

"I came to ask for your forgiveness." He passed her the flowers.

Afraid to assume anything, she asked, "For what?" Half fearful of his answer, she reached into the cabinet for a vase, added water at the sink, then returned to the bar and began arranging the flowers.

He sipped at his coffee. "It didn't occur to me until our discussion how you might feel about me living in Holt Ridge."

She added a rose to the vase.

"I didn't intend to invade your space, Lauren. The thought that I might be hadn't crossed my mind." He dragged a thumb over his mug. "Maybe it should have, but it didn't."

"I was surprised, I have to say." She snipped the stem and placed another rose.

"Okay, look. I blew it on two fronts," he said. "Cut the next stem a little shorter."

She nodded. Left it longer.

"First front, I didn't look at me living here through your eyes. You say it isn't why you stayed away, but that's what everyone thought."

"I told you. I didn't know you were here."

"I know that now, but then, I didn't, and I wondered for a good reason."

"What good reason?"

"I made your mother promise not to tell you." He dropped his gaze to the flowers.

"But you never thought she'd actually do it—not tell me, I mean."

His face reddened. "I guess I was more persuasive than I thought."

"Persuasive?" Now that was an interesting response. Another flower into the vase. More jammed in than placed.

"That's my fault, too," he confessed. "I told her you'd built a happy life for yourself without me in Atlanta."

Lauren stilled. "How would you know that?"

Ignoring her question, he went on. "I also told her, after what I'd done, I had no right to disrupt your life again."

Convinced, Lauren's skin prickled. "You watched me in Atlanta?"

"I watched over you," he corrected her. "Big difference."

"Seriously?" She forgot about messing with the flowers and glared at him. "I don't think so."

"Rethink," he suggested. "Your mom was worried, Lauren. You hadn't returned here even once. You were, according to her, deliberately evasive about your life there. She loves you. Of course, she was worried."

She probably had been.

"When I told her you were dating intermittently, she was relieved, and she was happy for you when you started seeing James."

He knew too much. Enough to know she wasn't seriously involved with anyone, including James. "Sounds like a violation of privacy from where I'm standing."

"It wasn't like that, I promise. I checked just enough to assure her that you were fine. Honestly, I'd hoped often that you'd find someone special and be happy."

Her heart skipped a wild beat and dropped. Pain filled the space. Why had he come here, insinuated himself into her life only to want her pawned off on someone else?

It was three years ago all over again.

She dumped the rest of the flowers into the vase and moved it down the breakfast bar, further away from her. "I understand," she said, her voice frostier than the air outside. "You're forgiven. Thank you for the roses. Now, it's time for you to go."

"But I haven't..."

"I need to get to the hospital, David. You've had years to say anything you wanted to say, and you said nothing." Oh, he'd seen the messages on her phone all right. "For the record, I haven't found someone special in Atlanta and I am far from happy there. But I'm making a life. I'm trying. So, there's no need for you to watch over me anymore." She put her coffee cup into the sink. "I've got a full day. You do need to go now."

Defeated and maybe a little baffled, and definitely a lot disappointed, David respected her wishes and silently left the kitchen and then her home.

When the front door closed, Lauren sat down at the bar, torn between fury and indulging in a pity party.

Caroline walked in and poured herself a cup of coffee. "Lauren, you know I love you, right?"

"Yeah, I know." She swallowed a heartfelt sigh. "I love you, too."

"I remember our pact not to stick our noses into each other's business. It's been in place a long time and I haven't violated it. But I can't stay out of this one. It's too important."

"What is this one?"

"David." Caroline leaned a hip against the counter. "I couldn't help but hear it all, and, Lauren, you are making a huge mistake."

"Don't go there," Lauren warned her sister. "You don't understand."

"I understand perfectly. You are the one who is bumbling around clueless." Caroline pursed her lips and swiped a hand through her hair. "David told you about his injury, right? I mean, you have noticed the cane."

"He got hurt on a job."

"Did he tell you how extensive the damage was?"

She shrugged. "He mentioned having a few surgeries, but that's all."

"Good grief. Well, no wonder." Caroline rolled her eyes back in her head. "Look, Lauren, you need to talk to him. No dancing around, just straight, plain talk. It's important."

"You seem to know a lot I don't. Why don't you tell me?"

"It's his story to tell, and he needs to tell it to you."

Caroline took her coffee and left the kitchen.

Lauren sat at the bar as torn and confused as ever. Her feelings were so mixed up on all of this, she couldn't be more divided inside if she had two personalities. So, he had a story, and the answers.

She worked through all the mental gymnastics of asking him, not asking him; talking straight and plain and saying not a word; and an hour later, she found the bottom line.

Heaven help her. No matter what his answers were, nothing he could say or not say would change a thing.

That truth washed through her like the current crashing water over rocks in the stream.

She thought back to the night before. The way he'd held her hand in the sleigh, the tenderness in his eyes, their kisses… And the one thing she hadn't done after getting into bed that was different from any other night in the past three years flashed through her mind, and stuck.

She hadn't listened to his voice mail. And she hadn't read his text.

Going perfectly still, she didn't so much as blink. Another truth rushed through her. She still loved him as much as she ever had loved him.

And he had hoped often to pawn her off on another man.

She squeezed her eyes shut.

When Caroline came back into the kitchen for a refill, Lauren seized the moment. "Does David still love me?"

Caroline didn't pause pouring. "There's only one way to find out." She slid the pot back into place. "Ask him."

The challenge in her voice was clear. It wasn't what Lauren wanted to hear, but it clearly was all Caroline was going to give her.

Lauren slid off the stool. "I've got to get to the hospital."

"Then the Community—"

"Yes, yes." Lauren shushed her sister with a wave of her hand. "I'll be back in time to dress for the dance."

"I'm skipping it."

Lauren turned and glared at her sister. "You are *not* skipping it. You're going to be there and keep Rory civil and I won't hear another word about it, Caroline. And I mean it."

"Oh, all right. All right." She frowned. "Get the thorn out of your paw. I'll go. I won't like it, but I'll go."

Lauren sniffed. "Frankly, sister, I don't care right now what you like or don't. I need you there, and you owe me."

"True. You've done the lion's share of all this. So, I guess I do owe you. But don't think for a second, I don't know if I answered your questions about David, you'd be a lot nicer to me right now."

Lauren grunted. "Right now? Doubtful."

"You always did hate being confused."

She had. Still did. So she ignored the comment and headed down the hallway to her bedroom to dress.

"Attitude is everything!" Caroline shouted through her closed door.

Lauren rolled her eyes and said not a word. She hated it when Caroline was right and left Lauren with no defense.

20

December 23rd
10:30 AM

IN THE HOSPITAL PARKING LOT, Lauren's phone rang. She didn't recognize the number. "Hello."

"Lauren, it's Mom."

Whose phone was she using? What had happened to her phone? "Good morning. I heard the good news." She cut off the engine.

"What good news?"

"Your meds kicked in and you've turned the corner."

"True. True. That's why I'm calling."

"Okay." Lauren reached for her handbag.

"Don't fret. I'm calling to tell you to go ahead with your day. I know it's crazy busy, with the dance tonight. Don't bother stopping by here. I'm going to have a shower and get my hair done."

"You are feeling a lot better."

"The difference is amazing." She laughed. "Just, if you have time, drop by after you're dressed for the dance. I want to see you all dressed up."

She always had loved seeing her or Caroline dressed up. Lauren smiled and fished her lipstick from the side pocket of her purse. "Okay. I can do that."

"I know you'll look lovely."

"Thanks, Mom." Lauren looked out the window. "Did you get the pictures I sent of the parade and the bonfire?"

"Not yet," she said. "Last night, everyone on the Ridge was sending me video clips and photos. Becky Grayson got so annoyed with my phone pinging, she confiscated it." Her mother sniffed. "She said it was disturbing the other patients, but I'm thinking she just wanted to see everything first."

That explained the phone. "So how are you calling me?"

"I borrowed Jason's," her mother said. "You know Jason, Jessica's—"

"I do, yes."

"Who would ever have thought our Jessica would fall in love with a truck-driving cowboy?"

Not at all surprised her mother knew about that, Lauren asked, "How long is your phone going to be confiscated?"

"Just until Jessica gets here in a few minutes. She'll give it back to me. Isn't it ridiculous that Becky took it?"

"She'll probably take it again tonight." Unless Lauren was dead wrong, her mother would get even more videos and photos from the dinner and dance."

"Not if she doesn't know I have it back. Jason's getting me a substitute. Becky won't get one call or picture to look at on it. He showed me how to turn off the bell, too. So, she won't know I have it back." Her mother laughed. "Clever, our Jason."

The sound of her laughter was magical to Lauren's ears. "Very clever," she said, tearing up. She would recover.

"I heard you and David took a little sleigh ride last night."

"Bailey insisted."

"Did he insist on you two kissing, too? Twice?"

Barbara Pope. Lauren should stitch her mouth closed. "No, Bailey didn't know about that until it happened," she said. "Actually, neither did I."

"Not what I heard."

Here it came. Lauren swiped on lipstick, then dropped the tube back into her handbag.

"I heard you bartered a kiss for a jar of Liz Baker's apple butter—for David."

"I did." No sense lying about it. "He loves it, and I got caught up in the moment."

"You don't sound very happy about it."

"It's fine. I'm fine."

"Lauren, your whole life, any time you say you're fine, you're a wreck."

Did she? Probably so. "What can I say? I'm a wreck."

"Why, dear? From all reports, you and David have been getting along really well. Far better than anyone—especially you, I'm sure—expected."

"That's the problem."

"Oh, my."

"What?" Lauren draped a hand over the steering wheel.

"It's occurred to you that you still love him." Her voice was maddeningly neutral. "Not surprising."

"Maybe not to you." Lauren grunted. "It gob-smacked me."

"Why? You did almost marry the man."

"And he ditched me." She blinked hard, fighting back tears. She'd shed enough last night to last a lifetime and promised herself not another one would fall today. "Letting this happen again… What kind of fool am I?"

"A brave one."

"Trust me, Mom, I am not brave."

"You're the bravest woman I know," she countered. "Now, the aide is here to take me for my bath." A pause, then her mother added, "Lauren, think about what you said. We'll talk more when you come this evening."

"Okay."

"No, not okay. Promise me."

She knew her daughter only too well. "I promise. I'll think about it."

"Good. See you this evening, dear."

Lauren cycled off her phone and dumped it into her handbag, shutting off the conversation in her mind. "Where to next?" she asked herself.

Community Hall. No doubt the preparations were well underway, but she should check on them. The hard part? David was certain to be there.

"Just deal with it," she mumbled to herself then issued a warning she so didn't want to hear, she couldn't speak it aloud.

Act Two of *dealing and coping and struggling to forget* was about to begin…

21

December 23rd
6:30 PM

LAUREN SMOOTHED HER DRESS, took in a deep breath, then entered her mother's hospital room. Sitting up in bed, she looked wonderful. "You've got makeup on, and your hair looks great." Lauren smiled. She was recovering now, no doubt about it.

"Well, I can't be at Community Hall, but I will be at the dance."

Lauren stilled. "How?"

"Virtually." She smiled and lifted her phone. "Rory is live streaming to me. Oh, it's amazing, Lauren. I'll see everything that happens."

"Rory?" For a recluse, he was sure getting around.

"Oh, he's quite the computer whiz," Vanessa told her daughter.

"I didn't know that."

"Oh, yes. He designs those games people play."

"Rory's a gamer?"

"Has been for years."

That was a shocker.

Oblivious, her mother went on. "And I have a back-up plan to keep Becky Grayson from shutting me down." She pointed to a laptop screen. "No pinging. It's like watching a movie."

"Isn't that something?" Lauren was moved by her mother's delight.

Her mother scanned her, from the tip of her head down to her toes. "I love the look," she said. "Your hair looks chic pulled back and pinned up." She twirled a finger. "Let me see the back."

"It's a simple twist, Mom." Still, Lauren twirled.

"It's perfect with that dress."

Black, shoulders cut out, a thin loop around her neck, with just a little sparkle. "I got it at Jessica's mom's shop." She always had the best designs. "I didn't expect to be going to the dance, so I didn't bring anything to wear."

"It's perfect." She smiled. "You look..." She swallowed, emotional. "So beautiful, Lauren."

"Thank you." Compliments such as that were rare from her mother. She was a fashion icon in town—part of her duties as a Holt—but Lauren had favored casual clothes. "I have to say, it's nice to dress up now and then."

"I expect you don't have many occasions to do that, teaching."

"Once in a while." She shrugged. "But I love what I do."

"I know you do, and the children are lucky to have you."

"Thank you." Another compliment? How odd...

"I have a few things to tell you." She dropped the

phone near her side. "First, thank you for all your hard work here. It means a lot to me that you'd step in and do all I do for these events, Lauren."

"It wasn't that much, and I could never measure up to what you do, Mom. You're an icon in Holt Ridge." How many times had she been asked about her mother? Been told about little things she'd done throughout the community to make lives better? Lauren had lost count on the first day.

"I've gotten videos and pictures and calls from so many people, telling me what a wonderful job you and David were doing. Recruiting Rory as Santa was a stroke of pure genius."

"No, Rory insisted on playing Santa." Lauren added, "Recruiting Caroline to keep Rory from being Grouchy Santa was a stroke of genius." Lauren laughed.

"True." Her mother smiled. "Anyway, I am grateful to you. And so is everyone else."

"It's been a privilege," Lauren told her mother. "I'd forgotten how much all the traditions here meant to me. You were so wise to put them into place."

"It was your grandfather's idea," she said. "We must remember who we were to appreciate who we've become."

"Or to regret it," Lauren said.

"Works both ways, which was I think his point." Her mother shifted in the bed. "You know, Lauren, inside everyone is a desire to belong. Even people like Rory, who hide from others most of the year, needs to know he has a place where he's known and accepted. That's what these traditions are really all about."

"I've missed them," she whispered.

"That's a good thing." Her mother reached for her hand. "It got you back home."

"Actually, you got me back home." She squeezed her

mother's hand. "I never thought of you as frail or vulnerable. When Caroline called, it hit me how much time I wasted, thinking you'd always be here." She sniffed. "I'm so glad you're better now and you'll recover, Mom."

"Regret is a bitter pill. Which is why we should live creating as few as possible." Her eyes narrowed. "And that brings me to David."

"What about him?"

"You still love him. Two kisses on the sleigh ride."

"I explained that." Lauren lifted a hand. "It was for apple butter, for Bailey to win the bet."

"Remember who you're talking to, dear." A lengthy pause, then she added, "I know you, and unless you still loved the man, there's no way you would have gotten within fifty feet of him. Not after what he did. You've always been quick to forgive, Lauren, but you've never in your life risked a second chance."

She could deny it, but it would ring hollow. "True," she said. "You're right. I do still love David. But he doesn't want a life with me."

"Back then. He didn't think he wanted a life with you. But what about now?"

Lauren thought about it. Wouldn't he have explained? He had seen the voice mail and text on her phone. If he wanted her now, he would have said something. He hadn't…but maybe he'd intended to when he'd brought her the yellow roses. She couldn't be sure, but she had shut him down. "I don't know what he wants. I do know I'm terrified of putting my heart out to him again and him stomping it." She paced a short path beside the bed. "I'm not sure I could take that twice, Mom. I'm still not over it from the first time."

Empathy flooded her mother's face, and then she hiked her chin and drew her shoulders back. "That's fear talking,

Lauren Holt. Fear." She let that sink in. "Let me ask you a question." Another long pause. "I understand it's hard and the risks are real. But is protecting a heart from what it most wants worth losing what that heart wants most?"

"I'm not clear on what you mean."

"Protection is a double-edged sword, dear. Isn't it better to face your fear and take the risk than to fail because you never try?"

"The misery…"

"Subsides," her mother said. "Lauren, love is too rare and special to squander even a miniscule chance at finding it." She blinked hard, then again. "The hard truth is, you never know when your last chance for love will be your last chance for love."

She'd lived love with Lauren's dad. One day, everything was fine. They were happy, building a content life together. Then an icy ridge road claimed his life, and everything changed.

"Take your chance with David, Lauren," she whispered. "Don't assume there'll be another one. That, my dear, is the pathway to regret unlike any I wish you to ever know."

She still loved him. After all these years apart. Lauren dropped a kiss to her mother's forehead. "I love you, Mom."

"I love you, too, and I want you to be happy."

"I know you do."

Her mother's eyes burned overly bright. She cleared her throat and stiffened her shoulders. "Now, you get over to that dance and dazzle that man." She tapped the laptop with a fingertip. "I'll be watching."

"You and half the county," Lauren predicted.

"Carter said tickets have sold out."

Lauren hadn't heard. "That's great news."

"Family, this year, includes the critters. We'll have to see how that works out."

Lauren rolled her eyes. "David issued waivers on that, too."

Her mother giggled. "He's such a soft touch."

He was. "He loves Christmas."

"Now," her mother said. "He loves Christmas now. Here, in Holt Ridge."

"Yes." Lauren draped the heavy cape over her shoulders and clasped it at her throat, then lifted her clutch from the foot of the bed. "In no small part due to you."

She smiled. "He did seem excited to find his Chrismon on the tree."

"It meant the world to him."

"We all want to belong."

"We do." Lauren kissed her mother's cheek, then left for the dance.

22

December 23rd
7:30 PM

THE TRANSFORMATION in Community Hall was everything Lauren had hoped for and more. Twinkling lights, the huge tree stuffed with packages underneath, the strands of garland and their dangling bulbs. It looked enchanting.

In a large room to the left, children played board games and Santa's high-backed chair sat on the far end. It was empty, but his stuffed sack sat next to it, and his laughter echoed to her. He was somewhere close. She peered around the corner and saw Rory sitting on the floor in front of a fake campfire. A kitten rested in his lap and the kids were taking turns petting it.

"The other critters are outside in a makeshift pen." Barbara Pope stepped up to Lauren's side, shimmering in silver that matched her hair. "Don't you look pretty?"

"Thank you. So do you." Lauren glanced over. "Mom warned me David issued waivers."

"He did. The children were elated—and don't you worry. I gave Baxter a good talking to before we left home. He'll be an angel tonight."

Baxter? Only if he was unconscious. "I'm sure he will be."

"He's in the kitchen with Kenneth. Kenneth insists we serve dinner promptly at 7:45. Something about the sweet-potato casserole marshmallows browning being perfect then and scorched any later."

"Ah. So, everything is under control?"

"Yes, yes. The teens are helping watch over the little ones during dinner and afterward. Clever, the high schoolers giving them their own space so their parents can dance and enjoy themselves, too."

"Who is minding the animals?"

"Reverend Wong's youth group," Barbara said, turning with Lauren to the main room. "Do you like the centerpieces? I winged it."

A red rose and sprigs of holly, pine cones, and a white bow. "They're perfect. All the flowers are." Lauren smiled. "You did an amazing job. It's beautiful in here."

"Everyone told me their favorites and I just put them all together."

"It's gorgeous. You're so talented, Barbara."

Barbara blushed. "David is sitting right over there." She motioned toward the left, near the center of the room. "He wanted to know the moment you arrived."

"Why?" Lauren gazed from the back of David's head to Barbara.

"Well, I guess he's just eager to see you, Lauren." Barbara smiled. "He has been waiting a long time."

"He arrived early, then?" No surprise there.

"You could say that."

"Guess I'd better go see if there's a crisis."

Lauren walked around the white-cloth draped table, spotted her name on the card beside his. He wore a tux. A black tux with a red tie, for the occasion. Looking at him left her breathless. He started to stand.

Lauren put a hand at his shoulder. "Don't get up." She took her seat.

"You look stunning." Appreciation shone in his eyes.

"Thank you." She smiled. "So how are we doing?"

"It's a win," he said. "Doesn't the hall look great?"

"It does." She scanned the full room, the soft-lit dance floor, the band on the stage.

"Did you stop by to see your mom?"

"I did. She wanted to see me dressed up." Her mother's words about taking the chance on David replayed in her mind. "Someone sent her a video. She really enjoyed seeing you find your Chrismon on the tree."

"That got to me." He tapped his chest. "I admit it."

It had. The way it'd gotten to him had gotten to Lauren, too. "We had a good talk about the value of traditions." She tilted her head. "You never know how much the little things mean to people."

"They're only little things to those who have them. To those who don't, traditions are huge things."

"Huge?"

He nodded. "Really huge." He sipped at a glass of wine. "When I found that Chrismon, I knew I wasn't an outsider anymore. I'm as much a part of this community as everyone else—well, except maybe for your mom, and you."

"You are," Lauren said softly. Belonging meant a great deal to him. That was evident. She was the outsider now. She didn't resent it. She couldn't. She'd chosen to leave.

But she could choose to come back and be accepted.

"It's special, having a place to call home that feels like home should feel."

"It is," she agreed, seeing Jessica and Jason make their way to the table.

A bell chimed.

The music stopped and the mayor took the stage. "Good evening, everyone and welcome to Holt Ridge's annual Christmas dinner and dance…"

David leaned close. "I hope he keeps it short."

"If he doesn't," Lauren whispered back, "he'll answer to Kenneth Pope for the scorched sweet potato casserole."

Their faces close, David smiled, and Lauren smiled back.

"Thank you, Lauren and David, for making all our festivities a success." He paused and waved. "And thank you to Vanessa Holt, who couldn't be with us tonight because she's still vacationing at Memorial Hospital. She's doing well, I'm happy to report. Vanessa, thank you for your years of devotion to all of us in Holt Ridge. You are indeed our beloved First Lady."

To deafening applause, David told Lauren, "That'll mean a lot to her."

It would. "For years."

"Holt duty," they said simultaneously, proving they knew her mother well.

"Merry Christmas, everyone. Enjoy dinner and the dance." The mayor wrapped up his speech. "And watch yourselves. Our romantic florist and friend has more mistletoe inside this hall tonight than Mother Nature has outside." He grinned. "You're a wise woman, Barbara Pope."

David lifted his hand. "Mayor!" He turned to Lauren. "The announcement."

They joined the mayor on the stage. David thanked everyone for coming, then motioned to Lauren to take the microphone. "You do it," he whispered. "Mrs. Wong? Where are you?" He scanned the crowd.

She stood up at a table on the right side of the room. "I'm right here."

Lauren smiled at her. "Mrs. Wong, you've been an inspiration to everyone in our community for such a long time. Thank you for that," Lauren said. "We understand you're working on getting your RN degree, and you need to leave school a few weeks before the term ends to do it."

"Unfortunately, I do." Clearly, she wasn't happy at the prospect, or of missing a semester of her job with the children.

"The nurses at Memorial have resolved the timing issue, Mrs. Wong," Lauren said. "I called Jessica Weaver and, in just no time, she had so many volunteers to cover the days for you, that you can take those two weeks as paid vacation and be back at school in the fall."

Mrs. Wong's jaw dropped loose. "Really? All two weeks?" She scanned the faces, found Jessica's and ran to her. "Thank you, Jessica." She hugged her hard. "Thank you so much. I can't believe you're all doing this for me." She drew back. "But what about the nurses losing their vacation—"

Jessica beamed. "The administration at Memorial granted paid leave to every nurse doing a day of volunteer work at the school. It's a win all around."

"Oh, I can't believe you people. The hospital, too?" She sniffed. "You're so good to me." Tears streamed down Mrs. Wong's face.

"You've touched our lives in many ways, Mrs. Wong," Lauren said. "It's a privilege to be able to do some small thing for you."

"I'm overwhelmed. Just overwhelmed." She returned to her table, sniffling. "Thank you all so much." Her husband passed her a tissue.

"Have fun, everyone." Lauren passed back the mike and she and David stepped off the stage.

"Now that is what life should be all about."

"She was in tears, David."

"Happy tears." He circled Lauren's back with his arm. "I love happy tears."

Two bells chimed.

"Dinner," Lauren said.

Little ones teamed up with high schoolers and made the loop through the serving line in the Hall's kitchen. In on the right, out on the left with their plates stacked high.

A bark sounded in the kitchen. Barbara Pope's eyes stretched wide. "Oh, no. I recognize that bark."

Baxter came running through the main room, dragging a turkey. A whole turkey.

Barbara gasped. "Kenneth Pope, what are you thinking? I can't believe you gave Baxter a turkey without deboning it!"

Kenneth blew out a forced breath that could raise an ocean gale. "I didn't give it to him, dear. He snitched it."

"Baxter!" Barbara went chasing after the dog. "You promised no theatrics tonight."

"Let him out the critter pen door," Kenneth called out.

Caroline, dressed as Mrs. Claus, opened the door wide, and Baxter made a clean getaway.

"Watch that turkey streak on the floor," Kenneth said. "Somebody put some cones down Baxter's path, so nobody slips and breaks a leg."

Paul Miller and Binks grabbed a mop and cones that had been pre-positioned in in the corner behind a tall plant. "Kenneth expected this," Lauren said.

"Actually, I expected it," David told her. "I was warned."

"By Kenneth?"

"Actually by Mrs. Claus." David grinned. "I think she and Rory have decided to ignore the clock and enjoy whatever time they have together."

That surprised Lauren, and yet it didn't. "Love doesn't tell time."

"I guess it doesn't," David whispered.

Seeing the orange cones tracing Baxter's path, Kenneth said, "I'll get more turkey." He turned toward the kitchen.

"Kenneth, wait," David called out. "How did you know Baxter would do that?" What he was really asking is how Caroline had known it.

"He does it every year at Thanksgiving," Kenneth muttered. "Rascal dog. I think it's the cranberry stuffing. Maybe the nuts."

"How many times have I told you it's the orange slices?" Barbara countered. "Kenneth insists on putting them in the cavity, knowing Baxter loves orange slices as much as he does peppermints."

That had eyes rolling and muffled chuckling replacing fears of none of Kenneth's mouth-watering turkey being available for dinner.

A group of young adults—too old for high school or the youth group—served plates to the adults sitting at tables.

"Who are they?" Lauren asked.

"College students," David whispered. "I put out a call on the Internet. They came all the way from Nashville."

"That's impressive, but why?"

"Extra credit for social services classes," he whispered.

"Though some just wanted to experience a small-town Christmas."

"Clever, David. I would never have thought to do that."

"I'm learning that if you just ask, often you'll find people willing to step up. They don't because no one asks."

She thought about that all through their meal. Twice, she made up her mind to—at first private moment opportunity—step up. But one moment and then another passed, and she just couldn't summon the courage.

After the dishes had been cleared and the music for dancing started, Kenneth invited Barbara to dance, and Jessica and Jason joined them on the dance floor. That left only Lauren and David at their table.

"I'd ask, Lauren," David said, "but honestly, the leg's protesting. I need a slow song."

The hard truth is, you never know when your last chance for love, will be your last chance for love.

Her mother's words raced through Lauren's mind. Before fear could rush in and steal her courage again, she acted. "David, I don't know the details of what happened to us or why you haven't told me the truth about why you broke our engagement." He opened his mouth to interrupt, but she lifted a staying finger. "Let me say this. I might not be able to make myself try again." He remained silent. "I don't know why my mother and the people here who were supposed to be my family and friends have welcomed you into their ranks—though, seeing how much they mean to you and you to them, I guess I'm glad they have."

"It isn't what—"

"Please." She shushed him with a hand on his sleeve. "None of it matters."

"It doesn't?"

"No, not anymore." She nodded to confirm it. "The truth is, I fell in love with you years ago and, regardless of what happened, I still love you." She swallowed hard. "Whether or not you want me—which you didn't—well, that doesn't matter either. I'll always love you, David."

His eyes bright, David brushed her cheek with his fingertips. "Before you say those words to me and I can believe them, you need to know the truth."

Her heart beating fast, she nodded, not trusting herself to speak for fear he'd quit talking.

"First, there's never been a moment since we first met that I haven't wanted you. Let's be clear about that." He dropped his gaze to the table, then looked back up at her. "I know you think my injury happened two years ago, right before I came to Holt Ridge."

"Yes." What was his point?

"It didn't," he confessed. "It happened the night I sent you that voice mail. The one still on your phone."

He had seen it when he'd borrowed her phone at the bonfire. And he'd listened to it, or he wouldn't know it was that specific message. "Your accident happened then?"

He nodded. "My injuries were extensive. The doctors told me I'd never walk again. Zero odds, they said." He let her absorb that. "I didn't take the news well. In that state, I knew the only thing I had a right to marry was a wheelchair."

"That's when you sent the text."

He nodded. "It took time to accept. Longer than I had, actually. The clock ran out on the wedding. I had to do the right thing."

"The right thing?" She frowned at him. "Abandoning me was the right thing? Shutting me out?"

He covered her hand on the table with his. "It wasn't like that. I didn't want my limitations to become your burden. That's why I sent the text. I didn't abandon you or shut you out, Lauren. I set you free."

"No. No, David, you didn't." A hard knot swelled in her throat. "No woman considers being dumped by text the night before her wedding being set free." Of all he could have said, this she couldn't have expected. "You should have told me."

"I couldn't," he said. "I know you. You would have stuck with me no matter what. I couldn't face what I had to face knowing you were with me out of pity."

She thought a long moment. Then another longer one. If their positions were reversed… "I understand why you did what you did, but that was my decision to make. You should have trusted me to make it."

"You would have stayed." His voice sounded tight.

"Of course, I would have stayed." Honestly. "I loved you."

"You deserved better. More than I was capable of giving. You deserved a man not looking at life in a wheelchair."

"I wanted you. On your feet or in a wheelchair—it wouldn't have mattered."

"It mattered to me."

"I see now that it did." He didn't fear she'd walk on him. He feared she wouldn't. "You threw us away, and yet here you are walking."

"With a cane, yes."

"How did you go from a man with zero chance of walking again to a man walking with a cane?" She sipped water to ease the ache from her throat. "Multiple surgeries, you said."

"Six, to be exact. All experimental and none of which doctors had a high degree of confidence would actually make a difference. But coupled with a year of intense physical therapy, they did, and finally, I stood up. Another couple months, and I took my first step." He managed a trembly smile. "The doctors were shocked. A miracle, they said."

The thought of him struggling through all that, day after day. It made her heart hurt. "So, when you got proficient on the cane, you came to Holt Ridge."

"I did. But you'd been gone for a long time by then."

"Yet you stayed."

"To reflect and for the quiet."

He needed to belong. To heal.

"I couldn't try to win you back. Not after what I'd done."

"You knew I would have forgiven you, David," she said softly.

He stilled. "The scars are horrific."

"And?"

"I wanted to be the man you remembered. Not the man I'd become."

Down deep, she understood that. Imagined how he'd agonized over two bad choices and no good ones. "What about what I wanted?"

David frowned. "Your mother and I have had many conversations about that. You seemed happy in Atlanta." He looked away. "You deserved the best. Not me. Not the remnants of what I was and would never be again."

"Is that all of it?" she asked. "Do I know the whole truth now?"

He nodded, not meeting her eyes.

She scooted her chair closer and clasped his face in her hands. "I love you, David Decker. I will always love you."

He dragged in a sharp breath and slowly let it out. "I've always loved you, too, and I always will."

Smiling, she kissed him and then wrapped her arms around his neck.

"It's true," he whispered at the cay in her neck.

"What is?"

"At Christmas, we do return to the things we hold closest in our hearts."

Her mother's words. Again.

"Thank you for coming home, Lauren." He squeezed her close.

"Yes, Vanessa." Barbara Pope's voice carried to Lauren. "She took the risk. He told her the truth. And from the looks of things, I'd say everything is going to be just fine." Barbara laughed, hard and deep.

Lauren snorted. "Did I tell you I found the plans in Mom's She Shack. She'd already done everything she had us do."

He grimaced. "Um, actually, that wasn't her."

"What?"

He hiked a shoulder. "I hid the plans out there."

"You didn't. You had no idea I was coming back here. I didn't even know it."

"When your mother got the infection, I knew you would come. Just as I knew she'd count on you to do the festivities and not Caroline."

"That explains why when I mentioned finding the plans, she was lost," Lauren said. "She covered for you, though."

"I knew she would." He smiled.

"How did you know she would?"

"Simple logic." He shrugged. "Holt women are notoriously loyal. They're trusted with secrets—even if they don't know whose secrets they're keeping."

She had, so he'd been right, but that didn't explain his

actions. “Why would you do that—remove the plans from her file?”

“To spend as much time with you as I could. I hoped…”

“For a Christmas miracle?” she suggested.

“Another one, yes.” He looked into her eyes. “But this has worked out better than I dared to hope. I didn’t think for a second you’d still love me.”

The wonder in his voice set her heart to soaring. Them, together, that was a miracle. The miracle of bringing home Christmas…

BAXTER'S FAVORITE

CRANBERRY AND ORANGE ZEST STUFFING

Serves 8-10 (without snitching)

Ingredients:

- 10 cups dry bread cubes
- 1-3/4 cups chopped pecans
- 1 cup dried cranberries
- 8 tablespoons butter
- 3 celery stalks
- 1-1/2 sweet chopped onions
- 1/4 cup chopped parsley
- 1 tablespoon sage
- 1 tablespoon thyme
- 1 tablespoon salt
- 1 teaspoon black pepper
- 1 1/2 - 2 cups chicken broth
- 1 orange sliced (or peeling grated for the zest, if preferred)

Instructions:

1. Preheat oven to 350°F.
2. Mix bread cubes, pecans and cranberries.
3. Butter a 9x13-inch baking pan.
4. Melt remaining butter and toss in the celery and onions. Sauté two to three minutes, then add parsley, sage, thyme, salt and pepper. Mix well.
5. If you opted for grated orange peel, add it to the mixture. If you opted for orange slices, insert them into the baking pan (or the turkey cavity, if you're stuffing the turkey).
6. Add the broth to the mixture and stir. Use a little more or less to get the dressing to your desired texture. (Go a little wet to allow for baking.)
7. Empty mixture into baking pan and bake uncovered about an hour, until a light golden brown.

Very Important Note:

If you have a pup like Baxter, remove him or her from the kitchen *before* you get the stuffing out of the oven, and keep him out until you've secured the stuffing. Enjoy!

SNEAK PEEK: DEEP FREEZE, STORMWATCH SERIES

PORTAL 3 NEWS

Darcy Keller stood on the side of the road in the blowing snow and checked her earpiece, watching for her cameraman's cue. He counted down the last three seconds on his fingers. The anchor at the station segued to Darcy for the live shot.

"A severe weather alert has been issued for our viewing area. Holly is the worst storm in eighty years, and she's earning the title," Darcy began. "Fatalities and extensive damage are being reported in Montana.

"This morning, an abrupt jog has turned the storm to

Colorado. Specifically, onto you, Portal. The weather is deteriorating rapidly. As you can see behind me, whiteout conditions are already occurring. High winds and a mix of snow and ice are making travel extremely dangerous and next to impossible. Authorities are advising you get where you're going now and settle in.

"For the last several hours, flights have been halted in Denver and diverted to Portal International Airport. We're about five miles from PIA now, and it's taken hours to get this far. All along our path, we've witnessed cars spinning and sliding off the road. An eighteen-wheeler jack-knifed near the intersection of Interstates 25 and 76. The driver is critically injured. Stranded motorists have abandoned their vehicles and are seeking shelter on foot despite being warned to stay with their vehicles. Temperatures are plummeting. We expect subzero within the hour. Roads are closed to all but emergency vehicles and will remain shut until after the storm passes. The National Guard has been activated to assist stranded drivers but, be warned, if the winds get much higher, they too will be sidelined, as will emergency responders.

"Over 1800 flights have been cancelled at DIA in Denver. Now, I've just been advised, the diversionary airport in Portal has closed. With over 5,000 stranded travelers, Portal International is well over capacity. Our crew has been trying to make the typically thirty-minute trek from the station to PIA for over two and a half hours.

"At the moment, authorities are uncertain how many are without power, though they expect the number will be extraordinarily high by tomorrow morning due to ice and near hurricane-strength winds.

"We'll be onsite at PIA—Portal International—with live updates as soon as possible. Authorities urge residents to exercise extreme caution. In all of Portal's recorded history, we have not seen a storm like this. It's critical to your safety and your family's that you listen to the authorities. Follow their advice. Hunker down, Portal. And stay tuned for the latest weather alerts.

"A personal observation: Conditions are already rough out here. They are going to get a lot worse before they get better. Avoid taking risks, check your emergency supplies, and stay safe. Remember, things can be replaced. You can't.

"This is Darcy Keller for Portal 3 News. Back to you in the studio…"

CHAPTER 1

Tuesday, December 17th
1440 (2:40 PM)

Why do weathermen and women stand outside in near hurricane-strength winds, blowing snow and ice, to relay Emergency Weather Alerts, reporting dangerous weather conditions, and urge residents to stay indoors?

Emma Miller stood in a cluster of stranded travelers staring up at the TV screen in the Portal Airport terminal unable to think of one good reason for a person to put themselves through that misery. From Darcy Keller's involuntary twitches, the ice pelting her stung through her heavy red coat and the hood covering her head. Worse, she was clearly pregnant. A couple standing near Emma questioned the wisdom of Darcy Keller being out in the storm, risking a fall or injury. Silently, Emma agreed. The ice was slick. The heavy scarf at Darcy's neck draped down the front of her coat, and she wore a hood and gloves and boots so the only exposed skin was on her face, yet the cold air fogged her breath to the point viewers couldn't clearly make out her features.

From the advisory, it didn't appear Emma or any of the other passengers diverted from Denver to Portal were going anywhere anytime soon. Figured. At least the plane had landed before the airport shut down.

Emma had been exhausted before getting on the plane, though the adrenaline rush had gotten her this far on the long flight. When taxiing in, she had spotted a hotel attached to the last terminal by a long breezeway, but odds were it was already booked or there wouldn't be so many people staking out sections of floor in the airport terminal itself. Every seat was taken and most of the floor, too.

She searched her jacket pockets. Found her phone and half a tin of cinnamon Altoids. No purse, no money, nothing but the clothes on her back and the ticket and ID she'd had the foresight to stash in her slacks' pocket before making the rescue attempt. Darcy Keller had been right. It was going to be a rough couple of days.

Emma walked on from the gate area, looking for a less populated spot with at least semi-privacy to phone in a report to Home Base. The second terminal was as crowded as the third had been, and the first, Terminal A, was even worse than B or C. The din of voices droned a constant hum that hung in the air. She pressed to the northern end of an area identified by signs as "the Main." It was a broad and expansive opening defined by overhead, tented awnings, a food court and clusters of shops. Midway through it, she spotted a blessedly empty alcove and ducked into it, then retrieved her phone and contacted Home Base.

"Silencers. Liz speaking. How may I direct your call?"

Seeing the young redhead in her mind, Emma spoke softly. "Liz, it's Emma." Why was the Director of Operations answering the phone rather than the receptionist, Billie?

"Are you on the ground?"

"Yes, but not in Denver."

"They diverted you to Portal, correct?"

"Yes. And as soon as we were wheels down and landed, they shut the airport." Emma scanned the crowd rushing the food court. "Any chance you can get me some transportation out of—"

"None," Liz said, cutting her off. "You've been diverted."

Spotting an older silver-haired man with a thick briefcase and stooped shoulders, Emma visually followed him from an outlying sportswear store to the food court. Definitely browsing. "We've established that, Liz."

"I don't mean the flight. I mean, we—Silencers—have diverted you."

Surprise streaked through Emma. They were reassigning her to another security detail assignment already? She hadn't yet gotten home from the last one, and it had been grueling. Hostage rescue operations were always rough. "To where?"

"You're there. Portal International Airport."

"Seriously?" More perplexed than anything else, Emma inhaled deeply and caught the scent of lemon. She looked up and sure enough, there was a vent overhead. Why anyone, especially in an airport, would mask scents, she had no idea. It was a prime violation of protocol and an opportunity for unsavory types to insert bio-contaminates.

"Seriously," Liz said. "Look at it this way. You're stuck there anyway. At least you'll be busy during the storm."

"There are thousands of people crammed into this

facility, Liz. Surely PIA has its own security team." Every international airport did these days.

"It does," she agreed. "But your assignment isn't to secure the facility or the people."

That disclosure made Emma's mission as clear as mud. Briefcase Man reappeared with coffee and a pretzel. "What am I securing then?" Emma couldn't imagine.

"Just let me tell you, okay? I'm slammed here today—Billie is out until God knows when with the flu—so I need to streamline for efficiency."

Emma didn't sigh. She wanted to, but she didn't. "Fine. Go ahead."

"Use your same cover. Investigative journalist for American National Reporters—and no Loeb Award nominations this time. The director is still freaking out over the notoriety on your first mission."

Emma nearly had been booted from Silencers' training program over that. Security Specialists were most effective if forgettable and unnoticed. According to Liz, Emma's looks were Strike One against her. The award nomination, a huge Strike Two. If she got a Third Strike, she would be kicked out of the program. It was that simple. Everything she'd been working toward these past three years would be gone in a snap. No discussion. No reprieve. And no exceptions. Her fingers curled tightly around the phone. "I understand."

"Stay put under the tent in The Main. That's an area with stretched canvas overhead in the main terminal."

She'd seen the signs. "I'm there now."

"Good." Liz sounded relieved further explanation was unnecessary. "Apparently, a lot of construction's going on there."

"Noted that on the way in. Looks especially comprehensive on Levels Three and Four."

"It is, or so we're told. Heavy renovations. Fortunately, you'll be located elsewhere in the facility, so it shouldn't be an issue."

Regardless of where you were located in the facility, those open construction areas created worrisome vulnerabilities. Emma refrained from saying so.

"Your point of contact will retrieve you in fifteen minutes. Six-two, one-ninety, blue eyes, hasn't shaved in a few days, but he's a good-looking guy. His name is Dr. Gregory Martin."

Checking her watch beneath her black coat sleeve, Emma stilled. "Dr. Gregory Mason Martin?" Her throat thick, she waited for Liz's response. Dread churned with curiosity in her stomach.

"Yes, that's him."

A shiver coursed up Emma's backbone. Of all the people in the world, why him? The entire mission just wrapped up had been like this. She hadn't been able to catch a break with both hands and a net.

"Bio-containment expert. He runs the high-containment facility there that only a few know exists."

Emma frowned into her phone. "There's a high-containment lab here, in this airport?" What genius did that? Airports being terrorist targets had required they be hardened, but, good grief. Bio-contaminates in an airport? That was just insane.

"Afraid so."

Stranded in a wicked storm in a facility under heavy construction. Five thousand souls at stake, and now this. Bio-contaminates *and* Mason Martin. The news tumbled straight through bad and into worse. If not to protect the facility or people, why was she being diverted? "What's my job here?"

"Keep the lab secure," Liz said, then dropped her voice. "You know this doctor, correct?"

Another shiver coursed through Emma. "I do, yes."

"From a prior mission?" Liz asked, though she knew the answer already. Liz never asked a question she couldn't already answer.

"Actually, no. We grew up together and went to the same college. He knows me, Liz. My cover isn't going—"

"It will hold as much as is needed. His headquarters will see to it. This acquaintance could be helpful. If the doctor knows you, he is less apt to expose you."

"That's an assumption." Emma frowned. "He may be more apt."

"Oh, boy."

"What?" The scent changed to cinnamon rolls. She sniffed. Coming from the vent.

"That change in your tone. I only hear it when something is personal." Liz hesitated but when Emma remained silent, she added, "Were you engaged to him?"

Naturally, that'd be the first thing to occur to Liz. "No."

"Ah, so he must be the one who got away."

Surprise rippled across Emma's chest. "How do you know one got away?"

"Reasonable deduction. Anytime we talk about relationships, it's written all over your face," Liz said. "More accurately, it appears whenever we talk about the breakup of another of your relationships."

Emma clamped her jaw shut. Okay, so she'd been engaged a few times and had never made it to the altar. So what? Wasn't that better than a string of divorces? She opened her mouth to fire back a snarky retort, but fortunately good sense intervened. If she wanted to get out of training and off probation and be permanently hired at

Silencers, Inc., the last thing she needed to do was to cross Liz and lose her support. "No, he isn't the one who got away." Oh, Emma hated admitting this. "Speaking honestly, he's the one I never got."

"I see." Liz's tone held empathy, proving she did see. Too much. "Well, hope springs eternal."

That remark pricked deep enough to obliterate Emma's restraint. "Shut up, Liz."

"Ooh, Touchy." Liz sounded amused. "Significant sign."

Emma couldn't deny it. She was touchy about Mason. She always had been. "I'm sorry. Habitual response. He's totally insignificant to me now," she reminded herself as much as Liz. "All that happened a long time ago."

"Evidently, not long ago enough."

Emma bristled, stuffed her free hand deeper into her black jacket's pocket. "Excuse me?"

"The wound is still wide open, Em. It's in your voice."

Was it? Probably was. She denied it anyway. "It's not."

"It is. It's evident," Liz insisted. "But let's don't waste time arguing the point. Either way, never kick an opportunity to the curb. That door is opening again for a reason."

"Yeah, right." Emma rolled her eyes back in her head, stared at the white ceiling, blanking out old memories she thought she had forgotten. "He's probably married with a couple of kids by now."

"Mmm, maybe. Want me to take a look?"

"No!" Emma cringed at having elevated her voice and then lowered it. Fortunately, others hadn't crowded into the alcove, so no one had overheard her. "No, I do not." Liz bent the odd rule when it was essential to mission success, but to violate his privacy on a personal interest? That was unexpected. So was the temptation to let Liz look. Not that Emma would give in to it.

"Okay, then." Liz sounded unaffected, as if the offer had been a test. "Well, if you change your mind…"

Definitely a test. Thankful Emma had tamped curiosity and refused, she assured Liz, "I won't."

"Fine. But if you do—"

"I won't, Liz." Emma sniffed. "Some opportunities need to be kicked to the curb and some doors are best left shut."*

Coming December 12th

Preorder a copy of Deep Freeze

ABOUT THE AUTHOR

VICKI HINZE is the author of nearly forty novels, nonfiction books and hundreds of articles published in more than sixty-three countries. Her books have received many prestigious awards and nominations, including her selection for *Who's Who in the World* (as a writer and educator), nominations for Career Achievement and Reviewer's Choice Awards for Best Series and Suspense Storyteller of the Year, Best Romantic Suspense Storyteller of the Year and Best Romantic Intrigue Novel of the Year. She co-created an innovative, open-ended continuity series of single-title romance novels, an innovative suspense series, and has helped to establish sub-genres in military women's fiction (suspense and intrigue and action and adventure) and in military romantic-thriller novels. Hinze loves genre-blending and blazing new trails for readers and other authors. She is a former columnist for Social-In Global Network and radio host of *Everyday Woman*.

For early access to new releases and more, subscribe to the monthly newsletter at **http://mad.ly/signups/82943/join**

twitter.com/vickihinze

instagram.com/vickihinze

ALSO BY VICKI HINZE

StormWatch Series

Deep Freeze

Clean Read

Bringing Home Christmas

Clean Read

S.A.S.S. Unit Series

Black Market Body Double | The Sparks Broker | The Mind Thief | Operation Stealing Christmas | S.A.S.S. Confidential

Clean Read

Breakdown Series

so many secrets | her deepest fear (Short Read)

Down and Dead, Inc. Series

Down and Dead in Dixie | Down and Dead in Even |

Down and Dead in Dallas

Clean Reads

Shadow Watchers (Crossroads Crisis Center related)

The Marked Star | The Marked Bride | Wed to Death: A Shadow Watchers Short

Clean Reads

Crossroads Crisis Center Series

Forget Me Not | Deadly Ties | Not This Time

Clean Read Inspirational

The Reunion Collection

Her Perfect Life | Mind Reader | Duplicity |

Clean Reads

Lost, Inc.

Survive the Night | Christmas Countdown |

Torn Loyalties

Clean Read Inspirational

War Games Series

Body Double | Double Vision | Double Dare | Smokescreen: Total Recall | Kill Zone

General Audience (out of print)

The Lady Duo

Lady Liberty | Lady Justice

General Audience

Military

Shades of Gray | Acts of Honor | All Due Respect

General Audience

Paranormal Romantic Suspense

Legend of the Mist | Maybe This Time

General Audience

Seascape Novels

Beyond the Misty Shore | Upon a Mystic Tide |

Beside a Dreamswept Sea

General Audience

Other

Girl Talk: Letters Between Friends **|** My Imperfect Valentine | Invitation to a Murder | Bulletproof | The Madonna Key (series co-creator) | Before the White Rose | Invidia

Multiple-Author Collections

Dangerous Desires | My Evil Valentine | Risky Brides | Smart Women and Dangerous Men | Christmas Heroes | Love is Murder | Cast of Characters | A Message from Cupid Seeing Fireworks

Nonfiction Books

In Case of Emergency: What You Need to Know When I Can't Tell You | One Way to Write a Novel | Writing in the Fast Lane | All About Writing to Sell |

Mistakes Writers Make and How-To Avoid Them

For a complete listing visit http://vickihinze.com/books

Made in the USA
Monee, IL
28 April 2020

27318257R00111